BOOKS BY NELLE L'AMOUR

Secrets and Lies

Sex, Lies & Lingerie

Sex, Lust & Lingerie

Sex, Love & Lingerie

Unforgettable

Unforgettable Book 1

Unforgettable Book 2

Unforgettable Book 3

THAT MAN Series

THAT MAN 1

THAT MAN 2

THAT MAN 3

THAT MAN 4

THAT MAN 5

THAT MAN 6

THAT MAN 7

THAT MAN 8

THAT MAN 7

THAT
MAN
7

NELLE L'AMOUR

To join my mailing list for new releases, sales, and giveaways, please sign up here:
NEWSLETTER: nellelamour.com/newsletter

NICHOLS CANYON PRESS
Los Angeles, CA USA

THAT MAN 7

Cover by Arijana Karčić/CoverIt Designs
Proofreading by Virgina Tesi Carey
Formatting by BB eBooks

For every reader who has kept Blake and his tiger alive in their heart. Your heart belongs to me.

Whoever said that size doesn't matter needs their head examined.

—Anonymous

THAT MAN 7

Chapter 1

Blake

Ari Golden, the pharmaceuticals titan, sat catty-corner to me at my long conference room table. To the right of him, was my best friend Jaime Zander, the advertising guru, who handled most of Conquest Broadcasting's advertising as well as that of Golden International. Jaime was the one who had connected us, thinking there was a good fit and money to be made. I was at the head of the table, waiting for my wife Jennifer, the head of My Sin-TV, our highly successful erotic women's channel, to join us.

Drinking coffee that my longtime secretary Mrs. Cho had brought us, Ari's eyes bounced around the room, taking in the posters of our many successful series and movies.

"I'm excited to meet your wife," he said after a sip of the steamy brew, his gaze meeting mine. Just as he set down his cup, my wife dashed into the boardroom, breathless as she jogged over to the chair opposite Ari's. She was wearing a summery floral wrap dress that demurely showed off the contours of her slender but sexy, toned body. She threw her stuffed backpack on the floor and, upon sitting down, lifted her tortoise-shell eyeglasses to her head, a small gesture that always gave my cock a little jolt. Her gorgeous emerald green eyes met mine, then Jaime's.

"Hi, Blake . . . Jaime. Sorry I'm a little late. I was putting out a fire on the set of *Well Hung.*"

"I hope you called 911," I deadpanned.

Ari's brows lifted with amusement while Jaime stifled a chuckle. Lauren Blakely's popular romcom was the latest bestselling erotic romance novel to be turned into a made-for My Sin-TV movie. These steamy chick flicks had proven to be extremely successful, helping to bring the price of Conquest Broadcasting stock to an all-time high.

"So what exactly was the problem?" I asked.

"The actor playing the part of Wyatt couldn't get an erection on cue. After five takes, we finally had to give him a little 'assistance.'"

With a smirk, I rolled my eyes. This frequently happened. The problem could usually be solved with a little dose of Viagra or porn, and if neither of those worked, there was always the sock puppet.

Fortunately, that was never my problem. Mr. Burns, as I affectionately called my cock, never had a performance problem, especially with my sexy as sin wife. In fact, he could likely win an Emmy for Best Performer in the Sack. Make that in the world.

"I wish I had those kinds of problems," commented Ari, his eyes on my wife. "In the pharmaceuticals business, we have a whole different set of 'ups and downs,' no pun intended."

"I bet," laughed Jennifer, warming to Ari. My eyes stayed on him as he stood and rounded the table to shake my tiger's hand.

A little older than me . . . thirty-five according to the research I'd done . . . the Fortune 500 mogul was blond, bronzed, and blue-eyed and wearing a five thousand dollar Brioni suit that rivaled mine. With a commanding presence and his over six foot athletic frame, he was movie star handsome. I'm talking Chris Hemsworth handsome, and seriously, the two could have been separated at birth.

"So nice to meet you, Jennifer." His voice was deep and velvety and matched the seductive smile on his handsome face. "Jaime's told me great things about you."

I felt that little green-eyed monster—jealousy— rearing its ugly head, but upon eyeing his gold-banded ring finger I remembered that the charmer—once one of Manhattan's most eligible bachelors—was a family man, happily married to a highly respected toy biz executive and the father of two children. As he held Jen's hand, I couldn't help noticing how long his manicured fingers were. That meant something else beneath his gazillion dollar suit was likely long too. I generally didn't make it a practice to assess other men's dicks, but without a doubt, Ari Golden was well hung. The green-eyed monster inside me grew bigger and greener. When it came to my tiger, I was possessive—and protective—to the point of doing some serious damage.

I cleared my throat. "Let's get down to business, shall we?"

"Good idea." Ari nodded, finally returning to his seat. His gaze darted to me, then returned to Jennifer.

Take your eyes off of her, hot shot. She belongs to me! Inhaling a breath through my nose, I willed myself to calm down as a jean-clad Jaime chimed in.

"Blake, Jen . . . as you know, Golden International's breakthrough skin-care product, Dermadoo, has been a worldwide phenomenon. In part, thanks to the advertising campaign ZAP! created." ZAP! was the name of Jaime's edgy and very successful ad agency, which now had offices in nearby Venice Beach in addition to downtown New York. My hands folded on the table, I watched as he manipulated his laptop, which was hooked up to the large flat screen TV on the front wall. All eyes turned to the screen as a commercial began to play.

Three stunning women, one Caucasian, one Black, and one Asian, all with flawless glowing skin filled the screen. Their lush lips broke into sexy, confident smiles as one of them held up a Dermadoo tube and purred the tagline: "Dermadoo . . . a little dab will do ya."

The commercial fading to black, Jaime hit the pause button and Ari stepped in. "After considerable thought and research, we'd like to integrate Dermadoo into your My Sin-TV series and movies . . . and in particular, we'd like to sponsor *The Sexy Shmexy Book Club*, the goal being to reach an older demographic."

Sexy Shmexy was the highly popular daytime talk show created by Jennifer, starring my oversexed octogenarian grandma and her wacky erotic romance book club. It had been on the air for just a little over a year and the ratings were through the roof, and not just with viewers 60+. My grandma Muriel was even more popular than Ellen DeGeneres and was often compared to her dear friend Dr. Ruth. Women, regardless of their age or socio-economic background, adored her.

My eyes lit up. I was sure Jaime could see dollar signs flashing in them. "How much are you willing to put on the table?" I asked Ari.

"Let's start out with twenty mill."

I thought the dollar signs were going to fly out of my eyes. That would almost pay for the entire production cost of the series.

Ari continued. "All we want is for an announcer at the beginning of each show to say: '*The Sexy Shmexy Book Club* . . . brought to you by Dermadoo.' And then for your grandma to hold up the product and say, 'A little dab will do ya,' before the closing credits."

My grandma was a lot like me. Or should I say I was a lot like her. Both of us could sell an igloo to an Eskimo and a dick to a dyke.

Trying to contain my excitement, I turned to my wife. "Tiger . . . I mean, Jen . . . what do you think?"

Only one word spilled from her kissable lips. "Wow."

Wow was right! Then one word spilled from mine: "Deal."

A megawatt smile bloomed on Ari's face, revealing his perfect Hollywood-white teeth. He stood up, then I did, and we shook hands. "Deal," he repeated before we both sat back down.

My eyes stayed fixed on him as he reached under the table and placed a large box in the middle. "This is for you and Jennifer. A case of Dermadoo." Reaching into the partially open box, he tossed a few tubes onto the table.

"Thanks," beamed Jen, grabbing one of the tubes. "I can't wait to try it!"

"Me either," I added silently. Anyone who knew me knew I was a total sucker for beauty products and loved trying new ones. Jennifer always teased me that I was way worse than any girl she knew. The ultimate metrosexual. I had an entire supply closet stocked with every beauty product under the sun and when we went shopping, I was like a kid in a candy store in a beauty supply store. Recently, Jen had made me donate all my unused samples to a women's shelter. A dozen large boxes ended up being sent.

"Hey, what about me?" asked Jaime, feigning to be the little boy left out.

"C'mon, Zander," replied Ari. "You and Gloria have a warehouse full! I can't afford to give you any more after this deal. I'll go broke!"

We all exchanged a hearty laugh and then I invited everyone for a celebratory lunch in our executive dining room. Both Ari and Jaime accepted, but my tiger declined, having made previous plans with one of her best friends.

Which was just as well. Because I still didn't want her around this filthy rich golden-haired Adonis.

Call me an insecure, jealous son of a bitch.

Whatever. Because when it came to my tiger, for better or worse, I was *that* man!

Chapter 2

Jennifer

Sushi Roku was our favorite sushi spot. It used to be located near the Beverly Center, but had moved to Doheny just off Sunset Boulevard. I was seated in a booth opposite my close friend, Chaz, and his fiancé, Jeffrey, one of LA's premier event planners. Chaz, a successful fashion designer, was the twin brother of my bestie, Libby Clearfield, who also worked at Conquest Broadcasting. Now, the Director of Consumer Insights, she was away on one of her many business trips, overseeing focus groups in the Midwest. Sometimes, I thought she spent more time out of the office than in it, and traveling so much did not make it easy for her to settle down. Nor did her on-again, off-again long-distance relationship with her boyfriend, Everett, a visiting scholar in France. They had been going together since our USC college days, but neither seemed ready nor willing to make a commitment . . . much to both Chaz's and my chagrin.

Platters of our favorite sushi rolls were already on

the table. Crispy soft-shell crab rolls, rainbow rolls, spider rolls, and more. I never knew how we could consume them all, but somehow we always did. Chaz and Jeffrey were washing their rice-covered bites down with a large hot sake while I stuck to some non-alcoholic green tea. I was prone to getting drunk easily and couldn't afford to be inebriated all afternoon when I had a jam-packed schedule ahead of me. After lunch, I had to attend a taping of *The Sexy Shmexy Book Club* . . . watch and give notes on the *Well Hung* dailies . . . do an interview with the *Hollywood Reporter* . . . and review some submissions for new program ideas. Plus, I had an all-important meeting with Saul Bernstein, the formidable head of Conquest Broadcasting, that I had to be totally prepared for. Though he was my father-in-law and I adored him, business was business.

Devouring the sushi, we caught up, with Chaz telling me about his latest collection and his upcoming feature in *Vogue*. The fashion magazine was spotlighting hot, young designers to watch, and he was among them.

"Oh my God! That's awesome!" I blurted, swallowing down a piece of the California roll. I often wore Chaz's stunning creations to black tie and red carpet events, wowing both my colleagues and the media. He also designed my magnificent wedding gown, which I now kept in an airtight box so as to preserve it. Maybe, just maybe, the little girl I longed to have would one day wear it.

Jeffrey shared my enthusiasm and then quipped, "He's going to be so famous he won't need me anymore!"

"Stop it, darling!" Chaz chastised. "And have some more sushi!" With his chopsticks, he playfully fed his longtime partner another piece while I took a sip of my hot tea.

I set down the small stoneware cup next to my cell phone. "I have some exciting news too."

"Jenny-Poo, don't hold back unless you want us to read your mind. And you know how much we *love* to play games!"

They did indeed. In fact, if it hadn't been for a game of Truth or Dare that Chaz had initiated during my engagement party to my former fiancé Bradley, I may have never met or married Blake. It was a dare—a blindfolded kiss with a total stranger—that brought us together. A kiss to this day I still never forget. Or regret.

"Okay, spill the beans." Chaz wagged a finger at me and grinned sheepishly. "I know . . . you and Blake are having a baby."

I flushed. It was nothing like that. For one thing, we'd been married for less than a year. Plus, having a baby with Blake was complicated on account of the partial hysterectomy I'd had before we tied the knot.

But it wasn't impossible. I'd hadn't shared the promising news with anyone . . . especially my BFF, Libby. As much as I loved her like a sister, I had to always remember: Tell Libby. Tell the world. She was an impossible gossip.

I cleared my throat. "No, guys, it's nothing like that. A big sponsor wants to underwrite Grandma's talk show."

"Who?" asked my companions in unison.

"Golden International."

Both Chaz and Jeffrey furrowed their brows with a who-the-fuck-is-that expression.

"They make Dermadoo."

"Dermadoo!!!????" they shrieked ensemble. "No. Freaking. Way."

Their reaction shocked me, and my brows shot up. "You're familiar with that product?"

"A little dab will do ya," they singsonged.

"You use it on your faces?" Both Chaz and his fiancé had flawless, youthful skin, which made them look very boyish despite being in their late twenties.

"We use it everywhere," replied Jeffrey with a wink.

"Huh?" Was I missing something?

Chaz held up a hushing finger to his lips. "Shhh! It's the biggest secret in the gay community! 'A little dab will do ya' . . . a guy can get the biggest, longest lasting, best erection ever!"

Jeffrey chirped in. "With just a little dab, you can go for hours! That's why it's always sold out and hard to find. The gay community buys it up like it's bitcoins! It's even secretly traded on some L.G.B.T.Q. sites. Some will pay hundreds for a small tube."

"Holy moly!" My eyes were wide with shock. I wondered if Ari knew about this added benefit and wasn't telling Blake and me about it. And I wondered what kind of erotic effects it had on women as I reached into my backpack, grabbed a handful of samples, and set them down on the table.

"Here you go. Some freebies." Chaz and Jeffrey made a beeline for them as if a bird might swoop down and snatch them.

"Bitchin'!"

"Just holding a tube in my hand makes me so horny."

"Me too, honey!"

"You should have Blakey try some."

Trust me, Blake didn't need any help in the erection department. He was humongous . . . could get it up with just a breath . . . and he could sustain his arousal for hours, giving us multiple orgasms of epic proportions. With aftershocks that could last for days. We fucked like bunnies so he said.

How could anything in the world make Blake a better lover than he already was? Wetness pooled between my thighs and hot tingles shot to my core as I pondered the question and squirmed in my seat.

The check came, and Chaz, despite my hefty expense account, insisted on taking care of it.

"Remember, Jenny-Poo, a little dab will do ya."

Blake and I had a case of Dermadoo.

I was going to do more than explore its effects on my complexion.

Maybe I could fit in a little tryst in Blake's office after lunch.

Chapter 3

Blake

The three of us ordered club sandwiches, sides of fries, and Cokes. We ate heartily and talked guy shit. A mixture of sports, politics, and Wall Street gossip. Despite myself, I liked Ari Golden. Super smart and mega rich, he was also philanthropic. He had started a charity called Meds Without Borders, which provided much needed antibiotics and other pharmaceuticals to impoverished third world nations. He'd spent considerable time in Africa and was considering fostering a young Zimbabwe boy whose mother had lost her life to Ebola. He was extremely proud of his charitable work, and I made a mental note to make a sizeable contribution to his foundation. When coffee and dessert came, the conversation become more personal and turned to kids. Ari and Jaime instantly pulled out their cell phones and showed me pics of their beautiful children. Jaime with his now two-year-old twins, Payton and Paulette, and Ari with his seven-year-old son Ben and six-month-old daughter Rosie. Before having met Jen, I'd never entertained the idea of having kids. Now a pang of envy shot through me.

"So, what about you, Blake?" asked Ari, putting his phone away. "Are you and Jennifer thinking about starting a family?"

"Yeah, it's in the works." I took a long sip of my coffee, not wanting to get into the details of the challenges we faced. With my tiger unable to carry a child, we were looking for a surrogate. It wasn't easy.

Suddenly, a familiar voice sung in my ears, cutting short my mental ramblings.

"Blakela!"

I looked up. Sprightly coming my way was my grandma. She was dressed in a powder blue jogging outfit and athletic shoes that she probably bought at Marshall's and wearing oversized rhinestone-studded sunglasses that she probably found on Overstock. Being a big star hadn't changed her one bit.

I stood up and she hugged me. Then, she focused on my guests.

"Jaimela, how are the *kindela?*"

"They're doing great, Grandma!" No one called my grandma by her first name, Muriel. She was Grandma to all, including her adoring fans.

"Oy, such *nachas!* If only my Blakela would give me such joy!"

I suppressed the stab of sadness I'd felt a few minutes ago by introducing Grandma to Ari. *Perfect timing.*

"Grandma, I want you to meet—"

"Vey iz mir! You're the famous actor! I saw you in that superhero movie. *Vhat vas* it called? *Aquaman?"*

Ari suppressed a laugh while I corrected Grandma. "Grandma, you're thinking of Chris Hemsworth and he starred in *Thor."*

Grandma dismissively flicked her wrist. *"Thor shmor!* They're all the same."

"Grandma, this is Ari Golden. He owns Golden International. His company manufactures pharmaceuticals."

"Drugs? *Vhat* kind? You make *marivanah?"*

This time Ari couldn't help but chuckle. Unpretentiously, he spewed the many over-the-counter and prescription-strength drugs his company made. "We also make Dermadoo," he added.

Grandma's eyes lit up like Hanukkah candles. "A little dab will do ya!"

"My agency created that tagline," piped in Jaime with a shit-eating grin.

"You're familiar with that skin cream?" I asked my grandma, not privy to her personal hygiene and beauty rituals.

"Bubula, vhy do you think I look so young? Not a day over thirty-nine!"

This time Ari could not stifle a laugh. "You look amazing!"

I had to agree. Grandma was close to eighty-five, but she looked a lot younger than her years. And she had the energy of a twenty-one-year old. In more ways than one.

"So you use it on your face?" I asked.

"No, on my Luigi." Interrupting, I informed Ari that Luigi was Grandma's husband. Actually her second one, but Grandma gave me no time to mention that. "It keeps him going for hours. *Kenahora!*"

"What do you mean?" Curiosity also washed over Ari and Jaime. They were all ears.

Grandma winked. "Just a little *schnitzel* on his *shmekel* is all he needs!"

Was she saying that Dermadoo was some kind of aphrodisiac? A sexual enhancer? The next Viagra?

My eyes swept to Ari. Like me, he was Jewish and I was certain he understood Grandma's Yiddish. He blushed slightly.

"I didn't tell you, Blake, but we've been test marketing a new product very similar to Dermadoo as a libido booster. Our company has gotten many letters and emails from consumers informing us of this other 'benefit.'" He put air quotes around his last word.

"*Bubula,* you should call it Upadoo. Just ask my Luigi. And *Oy! Vhat* it can do for the *kooshkas* . . . if you know *vhat* I mean."

She gave Ari another wink. Feeling my cheeks heat, I switched the subject before Grandma got into her sexual exploits with Luigi. The two octogenarians were lock, cock, and rocking it.

"Grandma, I have exciting news."

She dramatically slapped a hand to her heart. "I'm *kvelling!* You and Jennifer are going to make me a great *savta?"*

"Not yet, Grandma."

Disappointment fell over her. She palmed her forehead as if she had an Excedrin headache. "I should only live to be a hundred. *Vhat* are you *vaiting* for?"

I didn't answer. Instead, I told her about the deal I'd made with Ari Golden. Dermadoo was going to sponsor her talk show—*The Sexy Shmexy Book Club.*

Excitement replaced her disappointment. "So does that mean I *vill* get a free lifelong supply?"

With as much money as my grandma had, she was as frugal as they came. She lived for bargains and freebies. One of her favorite pastimes was walking around Whole Foods at lunchtime so she could munch on free samples.

"Count on it," Ari replied with a wink.

"Come, *bubula,* to the show. It's taping in a half hour. *Ve're* having Diana Gabaldon as our guest."

"The author of those *Outlander* books? Wow! My wife loves them. And the TV series too!"

Mine did too. In fact, Jen was obsessed with them . . . *and* the handsome Scottish actor who played the lead.

"Maybe I can get a signed copy for my wife," Ari hinted.

"Jen will be there. I'm sure she can arrange that," I replied before Grandma excused herself to go off to hair and makeup, muttering, "Makeup *shmakeup.*"

Finishing our coffee, we headed out of the dining room. Jaime went back to his office while Ari and I strolled over to the studio where Grandma taped her show. I thought about the deal I'd just made with Ari Golden.

And I thought about the case of Dermadoo sitting in my office.

A little dab will do ya. My cock twitched. I was eager to find out.

Chapter 4

Blake

It was a short walk to the studio where Grandma and her cronies taped *The Sexy Shmexy Book Club*. Ari and I were seated on high back canvas chairs, close to the director and one of the monitors. On the screen of the monitor, Grandma's set looked small and intimate, but in actuality, the studio was quite big to accommodate the thirty-man crew and enormous amount of equipment it took to shoot an episode.

The format of the show was simple. Grandma and her five opinionated cohorts sat around a table, heatedly discussing the book at hand, reading aloud favorite passages. Generally, these selections were either swoon-worthy sexy or heart-wrenching angsty. Then, usually, the author joined them and the conversation grew more titillating. And revealing.

This taping was no different. With copies of the books in their hands, Grandma and her zealous group had been joined by Diana Gabaldon, the author of the bestselling *Outlander* series, which had been made into a mega successful television series on Starz. It had been quite a coup to book the author, but my tiger's persistence and passion paid off. She was a huge fan of the book series and watched the hit show—which I wished was on our schedule—religiously. *Outlander*-obsessed. I could deal with that, but what really irked the shit out of me was that she, like millions of women, harbored a giant crush on the male lead, the Scottish actor, Sam Heughan, who played the love interest, Jamie Fraser.

"How could you have a thing for a man in a kilt?" I constantly niggled. *And a ginger no less!*

"He's so sexy!" she'd reply. Obviously, women around the world shared this sentiment, but this didn't stop my jealousy from creeping into every bone in my body whenever we watched the show together. Maybe it was time to establish some house rules. *No Outlander Allowed!*

The round table conversation thus far had centered on how the author had come up with the idea for the first book. Interestingly, she had always felt that her destiny was to be a writer, but she had followed a different path, getting a PhD in ecology and becoming a university professor. Finally, at the age of thirty-six, married with three young kids, her calling beckoned and she started penning what would unknowingly become a critically acclaimed bestseller. Now, a very attractive woman in her sixties with numerous books in the series and more to come, she was a multimillionaire.

"*Bubula*, everybody *vants* to know," Grandma continued, "how did you know Sam Heughan *vas* right for the part of Jamie Fraser?"

At the mention of their names, I felt my skin bristle. My stomach crunch. Jealousy was a motherfucker.

Dressed in a smart navy blue pantsuit and a colorful shawl, Diana smiled reflectively. "When I watched his audition tape, I knew it immediately. Within thirty-seconds. Without a doubt, he *was* Jamie!"

"Could you picture him in a *kiltela?*" Grandma asked.

"Your grandma's a hoot," Ari whispered with a low rumble of laughter.

"Yeah. You have no idea." I hadn't told Ari that Grandma had a big hand in getting Jen and me together, boasting to her about how big my *schlong* was at our first Shabbat dinner together at my parents' house.

"She surely could," came another voice from off stage before Diana could reply.

My eyes widened. Jogging onto the set, clad in a full kilt ensemble, was none other than Sam Hueghan. Jamie Fucking Fraser. My muscles clenched as Grandma and her book club members screamed with excitement, grabbing their handheld fans and fluttering them madly. Meant for heated moments, the fans, with their hot book cover models, were coveted by viewers. It was Jennifer's idea to monetize them, and now

Conquest Broadcasting was netting a small fortune from selling the fans online as well as other show-related merchandise like mugs, T-shirts, and signed books.

"Oy veh!" shrieked Grandma. *"Vhat* a surprise!"

Christ. This was a surprise! How come Jen didn't tell me he was showing up? And talking about showing up, where was my wife? She never missed a taping of the show. Worry flooded me as the tall, buff actor jogged up to Diana and kissed her on the cheek, and then went around the table hugging all the book club participants, ending with Grandma. They were all still shrieking and fanning themselves, several taking chugs of their bottled water like they were putting out fires. Discreetly, a stagehand brought out a chair so that Sam could join them around the table. For a second, I thought my grandma would offer him her chair and then sit on his lap. The uninhibited eighty-something-year-old was not beyond any outrageous antic.

The commotion died down and my mind went back to my tiger. Her best friend Libby called her Calamity Jen for a reason. She was accident-prone. Anything could have happened to her. Maybe she got into a car accident! Or a brick fell on her head! Or she fell into a sewer! The possibilities were endless. Unable to focus on the show, I glanced down at my Rolex. It was a quarter to three. The show would be wrapping in fifteen minutes. Where was Jen? My nerves buzzed, dread pulsing in the pit of my stomach. I tried to calm myself, a little unconvincing voice inside my head telling me that if something had happened to her I would have known by now. A text. A phone call. Something. I forced my attention back to the set. Maybe it was better Jen wasn't here so I didn't have to see her drooling over Heughan the Gingerman.

"So, *Samela, vhat* do you *vear* under your *kiltela?*" asked Grandma, drawing my attention back to the set.

A sheepish grin spread across the actor's handsome, clean-shaven face. Along with a pinkish flush.

Grandma threw up her veiny hands. *"Vell?"*

"I go commando," the actor said at last in his too charming for words Scottish accent.

"Vhat!? You mean you have nothing on underneath?"

"Aye, that's what I mean."

"Doesn't the *vool* scratch your *shmekel?"*

Sam's brows lifted. "My *shmekel?"*

"You know, *bubula.* Your *shlongela."*

The big star still looked perplexed. With a wry smile, Diana passed him a note. He read it and embarrassment washed over him before he chuckled.

"Oh . . . that! Actually, wearing a kilt is very liberating. And comfortable."

All the women shrieked again, this time in disbelief and demanding proof. I honestly thought they would attack him and yank off his pleated skirt.

Teasingly, the Scottish stud stood up, curled his fingers around the flap of his kilt, toying with the woolen fabric as if he was going to open it . . . and then sat back down. Thank fucking God he didn't flash his dick! The women moaned with disappointment before Grandma calmed them down.

"Sorry *bubulas*, time's up for today!" As the closing credits music began to play, she thanked Diana and Sam for appearing on *The Sexy Shmexy Book Club* and handed them token parting gifts—the show's signature fans plus each a dildo dressed up as a highland warrior. As Diana and Sam broke into laughter, another familiar laugh echoed in my ears. I turned my head.

Jennifer!

She ran up to me and pecked a kiss on my cheek. "Hi, baby!"

"Where've you been?" I asked, trying to mask my anger in front of Ari.

"I'm sorry. I got caught up in terrible traffic. There was construction everywhere and then there was an accident."

"Why didn't you text or call me?"

"I couldn't. I left my phone at the restaurant."

Both of us had a bad habit of constantly losing, forgetting, or misplacing our iPhones.

"I'm having a messenger pick it up and bring it to my office," she continued, her gaze moving to the set where Grandma and her gang were casually mingling with Diana and Sam. "How did the taping go?"

"It was awesome," interjected Ari before I could respond. "I'm thrilled Dermadoo is going to be a sponsor."

Between my worry and jealousy, I'd totally forgotten about the Dermadoo that was sitting in my office, waiting to be tested. I suddenly had the burning urge to drag my wife caveman-style by her ponytail to my office and fuck her over my desk. My cock jumped as my tiger's eyes bounced back to us.

"C'mon. I'll introduce you to Diana and Sam. I can't wait to meet them!"

Him, you mean. Inwardly, I growled as Ari passed on the opportunity. He had a plane to catch. We hastily shook hands, with me informing him that our business affairs people would be in touch with his within the next twenty-four hours.

With Ari racing out of the studio, my tiger took my hand and led us up to the set.

Grandma spotted us instantly. *"Bubulas!* Have you met Diana and *Samela?"* She wasted no time introducing us. I shook Diana's hand while from the corner of my eye, I spied goddamn Sam (Geez! That's poetic!), giving a kiss to my wife. Jealousy shot through my system like a bolt of lightning, making my blood sizzle.

I quickly intercepted it. "My wife enjoys your show," I said icily, my voice as cold as my blood was hot.

"No, I love it!" countered my wife. "And I love you!"

I love you. Those three little words belonged to me. *Only* me!

"Thanks!" gushed Sam, all fucking gooey eyed. "That means a lot to me."

I felt my blood pressure spike, my chest tightening. I was growing angrier by the second. More and more belligerent. Though she met and worked with famous actors all the time, Jen seemed starstruck. Her twinkling eyes didn't stray from him. "You're even more good look–"

I'd had enough. It was time to show my wife that I was her warrior. This was my territory, my battle-ground.

I cut her off. "Jen, we have to go. There's something urgent we have to deal with." *My deflated cock. And my shrinking ego.* With a hasty but polite goodbye to everyone, I dragged my tiger out of the studio.

"What's so urgent?" she asked as I pushed through the double doors that led us outside.

"We'll talk about it in my office," I grumbled, taking angry giant steps across the lot. Jen was practically jogging to keep up with me.

"I can't! I have a meeting."

"Cancel it!"

"Are you kidding? It's with your father! He wants a full rundown on My Sin-TV before his board meeting tomorrow."

"Fuck," I mumbled.

No one canceled a meeting with my old man, Saul Bernstein, the founder and head of Conquest Broadcasting. I repeat: No one. Not even if you were married to his son. Or was his son.

Dammit! The Dermadoo would have to wait. And so would the angry fuck.

Chapter 5

Blake

By the time I arrived back at my office, I'd shoved Sam Fucking Hueghan out of my head, yet I still couldn't focus. There was a big Board meeting with my father tomorrow morning, and I needed to review my presentation. But all I could think about between reading the lines of the spreadsheets was fucking my tiger. And spreading Dermadoo, the miracle moisturizer, all over my cock and her pussy. Our sex was already out of this world—stratospheric—and I wondered if it could get any better.

At five p.m. I canceled my weekly seven o'clock racquetball game with Jaime Zander. Not because of tomorrow's boardroom presentation; I had that locked and under control. I loved slamming balls against the wall with my best buddy. It released a lot of tension and I beat him most of the time, which meant he bought drinks and dinner afterward. But right now, a different set of balls were longing to be slammed around— against the taut thighs of my tiger. In my head, I could hear them flapping. Banging. My bat-size cock was already angled at attention and prepped to hit a homerun as I packed my laptop inside my satchel. I started to text Jen: *I'm coming soon,* no pun intended, but decided it would be more fun to surprise her. Usually when I played racquetball with Jaime, she went for a girls' night out with her best friend Libby, but since Libby was out of town on a business trip, there was no doubt she was home. On my way out of my office, I humped the case of Dermadoo that Ari Golden had given me. *A little dab will do ya . . .*

Leaving the Conquest lot at 6:30, I got to our luxury condo on the Wilshire Corridor a little after seven, glad that the rush hour traffic wasn't too bad. Tucking the box under my arm, I undid the double lock of the front door and then set my computer bag and the box on the entryway console. The lights were on and in the distance, I could hear a faint hissing. As I traipsed through the open plan space, bypassing the kitchen for a drink, Jen was nowhere in sight. She must be in the shower I thought and then I heard her singing one of her favorite songs—"Roar"—at the top of her lungs.

My tiger had an awesome voice, and this Katy Perry song always made me insanely horny when she sang it. The memory of hearing her belt it out for the first time during a business trip to Vegas soon after we met filled my mind. Fuck. She was so drunk and so cute! I was already so in love with her. As I flashed back to that unforgettable night, a smile broke loose and my cock flexed beneath my fly. Oh yeah! Mr. Burns was going to make her *really* roar tonight.

As I approached our bedroom, the pounding of the water ceased as did the singing, and I heard the shower door slide open. I stepped inside our spacious sleeping quarters, taking in the panoramic view of Los Angeles from the wraparound windows. Then my eyes traveled to the pile of discarded clothes on our bed. Jen's heels on the floor. Her jewelry on the dresser, including the sparkling snowflake diamond ring I'd given her when I proposed. The vision of her slick, naked body danced in my head, my cock ready to jump in and take the lead. As I stealthily crossed the room, I was beginning to feel like a cat burglar. Scratch that. A *pussy* burglar!

With a wicked smirk on my face, I cranked the shiny handle of the bathroom door and swung it open. The room was all steamed up, but through the haze I could see Jen. Wrapped in a fluffy SpongeBob bath towel that grazed her thighs, her wet chestnut hair draping her shoulders, she had a foot perched on the marble vanity counter and was slathering cream on her toned calf. Damn, she looked fuckable! Her eyes cast down, I snuck up behind her and looped my arms around her waist.

"Hey!"

My tiger jerked with a gasp and with a sharp flick of her head, her terrified eyes met mine. "Oh my God,

Blake! You totally freaked me out! What are you doing home so early?"

"I canceled my game with Jaime."

"Why?"

"I had the burning urge to play with you instead. I hope you don't have other plans."

"I did." She slid her foot off the countertop and stood tall, looking at me earnestly. "SpongeBob and I had a dinner date at eight!"

"Ha-ha! Very funny."

Though sometimes I had to admit I got a little jealous over my wife's infatuation with the silly cartoon character. Still standing behind her, I pulled my tiger tighter against me. The intoxicating scent of the cherry vanilla shampoo she used wafted up my nose, arousing me further. My hard as rock cock pressed against her backside, longing to penetrate her. Parting her slick wet hair, I planted a kiss on the nape of her neck and inhaled her.

"Mmm. You smell so good."

A little moan escaped her lips. I kissed her again, my lips brushing along her shoulders and then wasting no time, I slid off the towel. It dropped to the travertine floor.

Spooned naked against me, she felt so good. Her porcelain skin always glowed after a hot shower, but tonight it had a special glow. A titillating pinkish tint.

Then, for the first time, I noticed what cream she

was using. *A little dab will do ya.*

"You're using Dermadoo?" I said, reaching for the tube.

"Yeah, it's really nice. And it's not just for your face."

"So I've heard." A silent chortle vibrated in my chest as I began to massage the cream onto her shoulders, making my way down her back to her gorgeous heart-shaped ass. I was getting harder by the second.

"Mmm, that feels so good, Blake," she moaned, tilting her head back and closing her eyes.

"*You* feel so good, baby," I purred, my hands about to cup her edible buttocks. I squirted another dollop of the Dermadoo onto my palms and began to rub the cream onto her taut ass with a firm rotating motion. Squeezing and massaging. Another moan spilled from her lips. I was turning her on as I turned myself on. I wanted to fuck her in the worst possible way.

Taking a quick break while my hips gyrated against her, I squirted more of the cream onto my left-hand fingers and then onto my right middle fingertip. In one swift move, I plunged the lubed up fingertip into her backdoor entrance and as she yelped with a delicious mixture of shock and pleasure, I placed my free hand between her thighs where it roamed to her hot, soaking wet pussy. I caressed the drenched swells, rubbing the cream all over them, before focusing on her clit. I was finger fucking her in two directions. And she was about to come. Hard.

Her back arched as her fingers clung to the edge of the vanity and little, sexy garbled sounds clogged her throat. The moans morphed into shrieks and pants of ecstasy and as I brought her to the edge, she managed three words: "Oh. My. God." I watched in the still fogged up mirror as she came apart and practically collapsed in my arms.

"Oh my God, Blake, that was so amazing." Blinking her eyes, she caught her breath.

"A little dab will do ya," I breathed out. My cock was about to burst out of my pants. Thank fucking God, it was my turn.

As fast as I could, I undid my belt, zipped down my fly, and then slid down my pants and boxer briefs at last freeing poor trapped Mr. Burns. He was so fucking big, pulsating with need and anticipation. Begging me for relief. *Hang on, Mr. Burns! I'm gonna take care of you.* On my next rapid heartbeat, I flipped my tiger around and handed her the tube of Dermadoo.

"Baby, put some on my cock," I ordered.

Still flushed and dazed from her major orgasm, she wordlessly did as I asked, squirting a generous amount along the shaft.

"Now, rub it in."

Again without a word, she did as she was told, the fingers of her left hand clamping the thick base before stroking my rigid length up and down with just the right pressure. I hissed, the heat and friction driving me insane. I was becoming bigger and harder if either was possible. It was the erection of all erections. I swear I'd never had one like this before. It felt fan-fucking-tastic.

"A little dab will do ya," she murmured. I couldn't help but notice the fiendish glint in her eyes. Did she know what I knew? It was time to find out.

Grabbing the Dermadoo, I squeezed a generous amount on the crown of my cock and then fisted it with rapid-fire pumps while Jen massaged my sack of nuts. I was so erotically charged. And so close to coming. My balls were already contracting with that familiar tingling feeling spanning from my groin to my toes. But that's not how I wanted to come. I wanted to come deep inside my tiger.

"Baby, I'm gonna fuck you hard. Are you ready for me?"

"Oh, Blake, I want you so badly! Please!"

I loved that she was begging, but one question niggled at me as I continued to pump my cock. Where? My mind whirled with options . . . on the vanity, in the tub, on the floor? Then, impulsively without overthinking it, I backed her against the wall, smacking a hot, open-mouth kiss on her lips, and then lifted her up so that my cock had easy access to her pussy. She wrapped her arms around my shoulders and her legs around my haunches, hugging them with her thighs. Inch by thick inch, I buried my cock deep inside her—or should I say glided because she was so fucking wet and I was so slicked up with the Dermadoo. Let's talk about a smooth entry. Holy shit! In no time, I took her to the hilt and on my next ragged breath, I was pummeling her like a madman. I cupped my hands under her butt and she squeezed my hips tighter with her thighs, her pussy hugging me like a wet velvet glove as I thrust in and out of her effortlessly at lightning speed. It felt so fucking good and like I could last forever.

Dermadoo was simply the greatest sexcessory of all time! Seriously, it beat any battery-operated sex toy by a landslide. When the secret got out, Ari Golden's bottom line was going to go through the roof! The lucky bastard!

I don't know how long we'd been fucking our brains out when I heard Jen cry out, "Baby, I'm going to come!" All around my cock, she convulsed and her hot, sweaty body shook. The look on her face was one of pure bliss. On my next forceful thrust, she combusted with a roar that could be heard in the deepest jungles of Africa. Simultaneously, I exploded, shooting a boatload of cum up her pussy, the overage spilling down her inner thighs. My head falling onto her shoulder, I held her up against the wall until our breathing calmed and our heartbeats regulated. Finally, I lifted my head and our glazed what-the-fuck-just-happened eyes met.

"Jesus, tiger. That was insane! I don't think I've ever lasted that long! Or banged you that hard!" With one hand, I tucked a strand of her damp hair that had fallen onto her face behind her ear. "Are you okay?"

She nodded. "Blake, that was simply the best sex ever."

We'd used and enjoyed lubes before, but nothing was like this. Dermadoo proved that not all lubes are created equal. Nor are all cocks.

As she lowered her feet to the floor to a standing position, I slowly pulled out my dick. It was all slick and shiny, coated with a mixture of my cum, her juices, and the lube. And it was fully erect, as hard as a brick . . . ready to go another round. In my head, I heard a bell ding like one in a boxing match and in my mind's eye, I envisioned a naked Jen parading around the ring, holding up a big sign: Round 2. Victorious and proud, scorchin' hot Mr. Burns was in it for the long haul and not going down.

I don't know how many times we fucked. I lost count after Round 3. We did it everywhere, every which way. Only taking short breaks to apply more Dermadoo when needed. We fucked doggie style on the bathroom floor, then I helped her to her feet and banged her against the shower door, thankful the glass didn't shatter. Then, I ravaged her lubed up ass while she was bent over the bathroom sink. Each time, she was as ravenous and rapturous as I was, overcome with lust and need. My only concern was that the neighbors would hear us and call 911, but after the third time I stopped worrying. We continued to fuck our brains out, both of us insatiable and unstoppable. A chorus of moans, groans, grunts, and shrieks filled the air along with some breathy expletives and exchanges of "I love you." We savagely groped at each other, nipping and digging, marking each other's flesh and talking dirty.

At some point in our sexed-out delirium, I carried her to our adjacent bedroom where we fucked on my king-size bed. While she recovered ever so slightly from yet another epic orgasm, I dashed out of the room to fetch the case of Dermadoo because we'd run out. Digging my fingers into the box, I grabbed another tube.

"I love this stuff," I said, twisting off the cap.

"Me too, baby," replied my tiger, her voice a rasp. "This time let's put it all over."

Before I could ask what she meant, she began squeezing the tube and applying handfuls of the magical cream all over my torso and limbs. And yeah, my happy, happy dick.

Then, I did the same, slathering the moisturizer all over the front of her body. Despite the ferocity of my libido, I took my time rubbing it in, spreading it evenly.

Best of all was applying the moisturizer on the swells of her perfectly pert tits. Squeezing another dime-size dab onto the pads of my middle fingers and thumbs, I tweaked her hypersensitive nipples and felt the puckered pink rosebuds harden between them.

"Oh my God, Blake! I can't take it anymore." She flung her head back and bit down on her kissable lips. "Fuck me! Please fuck me again!"

All greased up from head to toe, I lay down on the bed, my head on a pillow, and positioned her slick body on top of mine. As I attempted to slide my Dermadooed cock into her, she teetered, rolling around and unable to remain still.

"Slip and slide sex!" she giggled as I tried again and again. Our contagious laughter didn't help.

Finally, I slid it in. Effortlessly penetrating her so deep I could feel her cervix. In unison, we uttered one little word: "Fuck."

"Hold on, baby. I'm going to give you the joy ride of your life."

With urgency, her hands clutched my shoulders, her nails clawing my skin like the tiger she was, as I gripped her hips and started to hammer her.

Her face hovered over mine, and our eyes stayed locked while our hot breaths mingled. With each powerful thrust, her body glided over mine, the slippery friction adding heat to what was the hottest sex ever.

"Oh God, Blake! This is so incredible!"

"I've only just begun. I'm going to give it to you harder and faster. The thrill ride of the century."

Without wasting a second, I picked up my pace. Pumping her so hard and fast I thought she'd get whiplash. Our rapid, ragged breaths replaced all words. I could feel a thick layer of sweat mixing with the lube. And inside her, Mr. Burns was bathed gloriously in her slick wet heat, still going strong.

Everything became a blur. I felt like I was running a marathon. A long fucking marathon. Blanking out all thought except getting to the finish line. The only thing I was conscious of, other than the woman riding me to heaven, was that at some point, day had turned into night. The room had darkened, lit up by the moonlight and the city lights that illuminated her.

Her face was impassioned, the beads of sweat on her chest glittering like dew drops. My eyes stayed on her as she heaved with each thrust, both of us gasping for air as if we were holding on to our last breath. Neither of us blinked as I feverishly brought her to her peak.

"Come on, tiger," I coaxed. "Let me hear you roar."

"Oh God, Blake. I'm so close," she choked out between whimpers. "So, so close!"

The only problem was I wasn't. To quote Robert Frost, I felt like I had miles to go before I came. Well, that's not exactly how the poem goes, but close enough.

Not slowing down, I suddenly felt all hell breaking

loose around me. Or more precisely, around Mr. Burns. In an explosive series of convulsions, Jen's entire body shook like an earthquake and inside her, my cock felt like it was caught in the fault line.

"Oh my God, oh my God, oh my God," she moaned like a record on repeat.

Trying to catch her breath, she collapsed upon me and then rolled off, leaving me bereft and unattended.

"Jen, are you up?"

No response. I turned my head, then nudged her. Her breathing even, a contented smile spread across her face. She was sound asleep. Down for the night.

Unlike Mr. Burns, who was still up. Like *really* up! Plastered to my stomach as if he was superglued to my flesh. Longing for a release, my cock was throbbing.

Unable to wake up my naked Jen, I managed to get her under the covers. Despite the warm summer temperature outdoors, our room was comfortably cool thanks to the central air conditioning. I threw the duvet over me, but winced as it hit my erection. Before I could fall asleep, I was going to have to relieve myself. Relieve the ache.

Clamping my hand around the base, I began to stroke my raging boner up and down, but even the lightest of strokes hurt like hell. Mr. Burns wasn't responding and I could almost hear him cry out in pain and frustration. I began to talk to him like he was my best buddy, telling him to relax and let go.

"C'mon, Burns. Give it up!"

Nope, nothing. Not even a single drop of pre-cum. My rebel cock wasn't listening. I'd lost control.

The pain was agonizing; the throb insufferable. I groaned and began to panic, my racing heart only making things worse. Then, I remembered my old man's wise words. *What goes up must come down.*

Trying impossibly to ignore my sorry-ass state, I closed my eyes, breathing in and out of my nose, hoping, praying things would return to normal.

It must have been close to dawn when sleep finally claimed me.

Not for long.

Chapter 6

Blake

The funeral chapel was packed. Not a seat was left vacant.

Sitting in the front row next to my tiger, who looked more like a black panther in her sober ebony dress and the black veil shrouding her face, I turned around and surveyed the crowd of people who had come to mourn my loss. I could barely make eye contact with anyone because my loss was so great and incomprehensible. And so humiliating. I had lost my lifelong best friend in a grisly battle. My partner in sex and crime. Mr. Burns. The pompous actor, Sam Heughan, had challenged me to a duel—a sword fight—and whoever won, got to keep my wife. I foolishly accepted, knowing damn well Jen would never leave me. But I had a point to prove and an ego to defend. And now I regretted my decision dearly. I underestimated him. He was fierce. He was fast. With one swift swipe of his blade, the swashbuckler had gone for my cock and as I cried out in pain, crumbling to my knees, I put my sword to his heart. The end.

Sadness pricking the back of my eyes, I took in all the familiar, misty-eyed faces. In the front row, sitting beside me and Jen, were my parents and my grandma with her husband Luigi. He happened to be my longtime tailor and regularly altered the trousers of my suits to give them extra crotch room—fabric that now bagged between my thighs. Impulsively, I scrunched the excess fabric, feeling nothing but my worthless sack of nuts beneath it. The void between my legs pained me terribly and I had to fight back the tears that threatened to fall.

Seated nearby were my older sister Marcy, my buddy Jaime and his wife Gloria, Jen's best friend Libby, her twin brother Chaz, and his fiancé Jeffrey. The only family members missing were Jen's parents, who were away on an Alaskan cruise, and my sister's seven-year-old twin boys, who didn't know about my personal tragedy. With her ugly divorce finally behind her, she felt they'd had enough trauma to deal with and didn't want them to have nightmares about losing their willies.

Behind them sat my colleagues, including my secretary Mrs. Cho and my loyal top affiliate manager Vera Nichols and her husband Steve. Knowing what was missing from my life, macho Steve, who still had his pecker, kept his head bowed down.

They were surrounded by some of the stars from our network lineup, including action star Brandon Taylor and tattooed porn stars, Pussy and Swell.

Gathered in the back were all the women I used to screw . . . my O.K. Corral as many used to refer them because all their names started with "K." The blond bombshell twins Kristie and Kirstie, Kaycee, Kristen . . . to name a few. Though I'd abandoned them all to settle down for Jen, melancholy clouded their eyes. Yup, they all remembered what it was like to get a taste of Mr. Burns. Only one of my exes, if you wished to call her that, was conspicuously missing. The bat crazy psycho bitch . . . Katrina Moore. On this very sad day, that's all I had to be thankful for. Mr. Burns was gone! I couldn't look down at my crotch lest I burst into a guttural sob. I'd cried enough, but maybe enough wasn't enough. They say *real* men don't cry, but now there was no reason to hold the tears back. I'd lost my manhood.

My watering eyes shifted back to the front of the sanctuary. Standing on the podium were two familiar faces. That of my rabbi and Reverend Dooby. They had both officiated our marriage. Rabbi Silverstein looked stoic while Reverend Dooby looked more stoned than ever. I think he was feeling a Zen connection to my missing dick.

Then suddenly, I began to lose it as my gaze traveled to the small pine box to the right of them, sitting on a pedestal surrounded by myriad vases of white flowers. About a foot long and six inches wide, it was Mr. Burns's casket. His final resting place. Struggling to breathe, I swallowed past the painful lump in my throat, grateful that it wasn't an open casket service. I couldn't bear to look at him again. All shriveled up unless rigor mortis had set in and he was still as stiff and big as he'd once been. Honestly, I didn't want to know.

Rabbi Silverstein began. "Dearly beloved, we are gathered here today to mourn a most upright standing *member* of our community . . . Mr. Burns, the former best friend of our congregant Blake Burns, whose life was tragically cut too short."

My heart clenched painfully in my chest. Indeed, Mr. Burns was the best and most loyal friend a man could have. Over all these years, he'd never let me down—no pun intended—and not even in death. Even as I was castrated, he stood tall and brave, never flinching at the tragic fate that awaited him. A true soldier. One chop and he was gone. On the verge of tears, I was glad Jen took my icy hand. The warmth of hers was comforting though it couldn't bring back my beloved Mr. Burns.

"I'll miss him as much as you will, my darling," she whispered in my ear with a gentle squeeze. I squeezed her hand back, acknowledging her words. And then a horrific reality hit me . . . nothing, without Mr. Burns, would ever be the same. I could never pee in public again without shame. Shower or undress in a communal locker room. Wank myself off under my desk. And way, way worse, I could never get head again. Or get laid. The days of fucking my brains out were over. A terrifying thought shot through me. Would Jen leave me? Find another man with a big dick to give her the ecstasy I used to give her? I shuddered, bathed in cold sweat. Though she vowed to be faithful to me no matter what life handed us, I couldn't be sure. Nausea climbed up my chest, clinging to my membranes like poison ivy. Puking was one sickening breath away.

The rabbi continued, praising my dick's size, prowess, and endurance. He recalled my bris right after I was born and how I'd made it so impossibly hard for the moil to circumcise me. Trying to stall him as he attempted to cut the foreskin, I peed all over his treacherous hands, then pooped and wailed non-stop for over a week. Dabbing their eyes, my grieving parents nodded nostalgically. The attendees chuckled nervously.

And then one by one, Rabbi Silverstein called mourners up to the podium to share their stories and sing his praises. The most moving tribute of all was Grandma's. Eliciting a laugh out of the crowd as only she could, she praised my God-given *shmekel*. "A schlong like no other schlongs. Just like his Grandpa's, may he rest in peace." Then uncontrollably, the tiny woman burst into sobs. "*Oy!* My poor Blakela! And now he'll never be able to give his poor *bubbe* any *kindela* . . . not even one little Blakela! Such *tsoris!*"

Weeping, she let our rabbi help her back to her seat as a new cruel reality stabbed me like a knife to my heart. As if I wasn't suffering enough, without Mr. Burns, I could never give my wife the baby she coveted. I heard her sniffling and knew she was thinking the same horrible thing. *No little Blakelas.* I entwined my fingers with hers, my mind at war with my heavy heart.

What had I done to deserve this awful fate? Okay, I wasn't always the best kid . . . I indulged in mean pranks . . . I cheated in college . . . I was a player and screwed a lot of women, but ever since I'd been with Jen, I'd always done the right thing—if you don't count Operation Dickwick in which I'd eliminated her douchebag dentist fiancé. But that was for the best anyway. Bottom line . . . I was giving, faithful, and loving. An exemplary citizen and a good man. Hell, I'd even valiantly saved my wife's life! Why me?

Then unexpectedly, as I became inundated with self-pity, a commotion burst out in the back of the room.

"You can't barge in here!" barked a gruff male voice. A security guard.

"Just watch me!" shrilled a familiar female voice, dripping with malice.

Every head whipped around, and I gasped.

Holy Moses! It was Katrina, dressed to kill in head-to-toe Armani and accompanied by her insidious Botoxed mother Enid. A toxic mixture of venom and vengeance poured from their eyes as they defiantly marched down the center aisle in their stilettos, not stopping as they reached into their monstrous designer bags. I blinked and then my heart leapt to my throat. They were brandishing machine guns! On my next strangled breath, they each fired into the crowd, the deafening, rapid succession of bullets flying everywhere. Terrified screams filled the air, and the sanctuary became pure chaos with everyone ducking for cover or running to the nearest emergency exit.

Katrina's murderous eyes met mine. "Blake, you fuckface, you're going to pay! Say goodbye to more than your traitorous cock!"

What was the crazy pyscho bitch saying? Before I could put two and two together, another round of bullets was fired. An endless, sickening *Pop! Pop! Pop! Pop!*

A long, pained moan and then I felt a puddle of warm liquid saturating my jacket.

I felt numb. Had I been shot?

I looked down, and my jaw fell to the floor as I let out a silent scream.

Oh my God! It wasn't my blood . . . but Jen's! Arterial blood, bright red with oxygen. Drenching my white shirt as well.

My tiger's eyes rolled back as she gasped an agonal breath and collapsed against me. I caught her in my arms as she slithered down my body, limp and lifeless.

She was dead.

Chapter 7
Jennifer

"Nooooo!"

Blake's terrifying scream roused me from my slumber. After all the sex we'd had, I'd fallen fast asleep and could have stayed in bed all day. I bolted upright, feeling the soreness between my legs.

"Blake, what's wrong?"

Blake was sitting up too. His face was pasty. A grayish white. Sweat beads clustered on his forehead.

"I had the worst nightmare!"

I rubbed his shoulder. "Tell me about it."

Over the next few minutes, I heard all about Blake's frightening dream. The loss of his penis. Katrina. The lethal gunshots. "It's just a crazy nightmare," I reassured him. "Let me kiss your dick and make it all better."

Blake shook his head, glancing down at the duvet. The thick bulge punching the Egyptian cotton fabric didn't escape my sight.

"Jen, I still have a major boner from last night."

"That's happened before."

"But not like this. Feel." He took my hand and slid it under the covers. Holy moly! My husband wasn't kidding. It was an erection of major proportions, curled against his abdomen.

"And it hurts like fuck!"

I tried to assuage him. "It's probably some extreme morning wood. If you pee and take a shower, I'm sure it'll go away."

Fifteen minutes later, after I made up the bed (something I still did despite Blake's wealth and daily housekeeper) and combed my walk-in closet for today's work outfit, Blake emerged from the ensuite bathroom. A thick towel was wrapped around his waist and he looked forlorn. I couldn't miss the gigantic bump that was threatening to tear through the terrycloth. His desperate gaze met mine.

"Jen, I tried everything! My dick was so stiff I couldn't even pee in the toilet! And then, I tried to wank myself off in the shower, but that didn't work either." A long pause. "Baby, I'm scared!"

I heard the terror in his voice. He'd not sounded this terrified since the time Katrina had drugged him at his former fuck pad . . . and he *couldn't* get it up. And now, he ironically couldn't get it down. I glanced one more time at his bulge. Eeks! Had it gotten bigger?

"Relax, Blake. Let me do some online research."

He plopped down on the bed, his eyes cast down at

his erection, looking dejected, and murmured, "Fine."

Shrugging on the shirt he'd worn last night, I grabbed my iPhone from the night table and typed "Erection that won't go down" into the Google search bar. Pages of entries came up. I opened the first one.

"Ice the penis," I read aloud and flinging the phone onto the bed, dashed to the fridge. Retrieving some ice cubes from the dispenser and wrapping them in a dishcloth, I hurried back to Blake. Undoing his towel, I gently rubbed the encased cubes up and down his majorly engorged dick. Blake hissed, the sharp sound more like one that emanated from pain than from pleasure. I continued my machinations for another few minutes. Shit. No reaction. Well, except for it turning a shade of purple and the vein beneath it thickening. My husband's colossal dick was still curled up like a serpent! "C'mon, go down," I coaxed silently, icing it some more.

Then, finally! Progress! It uncurled slowly from his taut flat stomach . . . but now it was pointing at me like a ten-inch torpedo! Ready to attack! Frantically, I iced it again, running the ice pack up and down his long, thick, rigid shaft, picking up my pace in utter frustration. Blake's erection didn't budge an inch. Not even a tiny millimeter.

"Baby, why isn't it going down?" he croaked, his voice shaky.

"Let me do some more research." Tentatively, setting the icepack on the bed, I picked up my cell phone and learned that Blake had a rare syndrome. It had a name.

"A petrified woody?" he stammered.

"No, priapism."

"Priapism?"

"It's exactly what you have. When your penis won't deflate."

"Jesus. What does it say I should do?"

I read more of the WebMD article.

"It suggests taking a warm bath."

"But I just took a long hot shower and it did shit. What else?"

"Ride your exercise bike. Or go for a jog."

"Jen, are you fucking kidding me? I can't do either! It's way too big and hurts too goddamn much!"

Silently, I speed-read more of the article. With each word, fear crept into my bloodstream. Nothing was working, and Blake had suffered this prolonged erection for more than four hours. Scrolling down further, I gulped. A prolonged erection could damage the penis and lead to permanent erectile dysfunction! Blake read the fear on my face, his complexion paling.

"What's wrong?"

"N-nothing," I stuttered, keeping my findings to myself and grateful that Blake wasn't breathing over my shoulder and reading what I'd discovered. "I think we should call your sister."

"My sister?" Blake gasped. "She's an OB-GYN. She specializes in pussies, not weenies."

"But maybe she knows someone who does."

Moments later, Blake was on his cell phone with his sister. He put the call on speaker.

"Blake, what's up?" Marcy asked, her voice clipped.

The irony of her words wasn't lost on me as my husband glanced down at his enormous bulge.

"I've got a problem. A big one."

"Can it wait? I'm running out the door. I have to be at Cedars for a C-section in a half hour."

"No, it can't wait."

"Okay, just tell me what it is quickly." Impatience laced her voice.

"Um . . . uh . . . well . . ."

Blake couldn't get the words out and was wasting precious time. I jumped in, grabbing the phone.

"Hi, Marcy. It's me, Jen." The slightest of pauses. "Blake's got an erection that won't go down, and he's in a lot of pain."

There was no hesitation on her end.

"Priapism. Jen, that's not good. He needs to see a doctor right away."

Blake was already pacing around the room like a madman looking for his doctor's phone number. Opening and slamming shut drawers. Turning every-thing upside down. Throwing a pile of bills up in the air, he yelled, "Fuck. Where the hell did I put it?"

My husband wasn't thinking straight. His condition was messing with his brain. Being the hypochondriac he was, the number was likely stored on his cell phone and he could speed dial Dr. Klein. I hastily thanked Marcy, wishing her luck with the cesarean, and ended the call. It wasn't even seven a.m. I handed the phone back to Blake.

"Here. I'm sure Dr. Klein is in your list of contacts." Wasting no time, he scrolled through his long list and then hit call. His cell still on speaker, I heard the doctor's office phone ring and ring. Finally, on the fifth ring, it went to voicemail.

"You have reached the office of Dr. Marvin Klein. Our regular office hours are 9 a.m. to 5 p.m., Monday through Friday. If you have a medical emergency, please hang up and dial 911. For all other matters, please leave a message at the sound of the beep and we'll get back to you as soon as we can."

Blake jabbed the end call button before the beep sounded and tossed the phone onto the bed. "Fuck. Shit. Fuck!"

Tenderly, I put my hand on his arm. "Baby, let's go to the emergency room."

"I can't; there's no time. I have my father's Board meeting this morning, and I absolutely have to be there. Board members have flown in from all over the world and he's counting on my PowerPoint presentation to wow them."

My turn to curse. "What are you going to do?"

Blake grimaced, part in pain, part in despair. "The bigger question is what am I going to wear?"

My brows rose to my forehead. What to wear was never a dilemma for Blake. My clotheshorse husband had a walk-in closet the size of a vault filled with a gazillion suits, ties, shirts, and shoes. All of them color-coded for easy access. His fashion sense was impeccable.

His panicked eyes shot down to his crotch and then back to me. "Jen, I'll never be able to zip up a fly over this monstrosity."

"Maybe you can wear a coat over your suit and hide it."

"All my coats are in storage and who the hell would wear a heavy cashmere coat in the middle of August?"

He had a point. "What about your Burberry raincoat? You can pretend you heard it's going to rain."

"Fat chance. The sun's already shining and it hasn't rained in LA for nine months. And besides it's at the dry cleaner."

My mind raced. "You could wear some loose sweats."

He glanced down again at his humongous erection and shook his head. "Are you fricking kidding? With this thing? It'll stick out like a sore thumb, no pun intended."

He was right again. His erection was so big it likely wouldn't fit under his father's conference room table. And what if he had to stand up, which usually he did? I put my thinking cap back on. *Think, Jen, think.* And then all of a sudden it came to me.

Fifteen minutes later, Blake was wearing one of his crisp white dress shirts, a beautiful black gabardine jacket, shiny leather loafers, dark socks . . .

And what my parents had bought him on their trip abroad earlier in the year.

It was better than nothing.

Literally.

Chapter 8

Blake

I was ridiculously clad in the red tartan kilt my in-laws had brought me back from Scotland. Yup, a fricking kilt of all things! But I had no choice. In my current state, it was the only thing that fit me. And fit *it*.

Jennifer stared at me as I stood before the floor-length mirror and adjusted the leather pouch it came with over my groin. I despised man bags, but this one was functional and it concealed my ginormous boner though it couldn't mask the acute pain I was still in.

My wife gave me a once-over. "Blake, I think you look incredibly sexy in a kilt."

As sexy as Jamie Fraser? I wanted to ask.

She smiled. "You can be my highland warrior any-time."

I did not return the smile. Instead, I made a face, my eyes trailing down past my knees, where the hem hit, to my hairy muscular calves. In addition to feeling extremely uncomfortable, I felt very vulnerable, one safety pin away from exposing my erection from hell. I wasn't wearing anything beneath the pleated skirt. My throbbing cock hurt too fucking much to slip on boxer briefs so I was going to work commando.

Dressed in a sleeveless A-line pink shift, my tiger looped her arms around my waist. Her body brushed against mine, skimming my hypersensitive groin.

"Ow!" I yelped as she stepped away.

"Sorry." She made an apologetic face, then gave me a sweet seductive smile. "I think it would be fun to fuck you in a kilt. Or give you a blow job. Or a hand job. I'd just have to remove the safety pin and simply slide my hand underneath the flap."

Under any other circumstances, I would have been turned on, but my painfully swollen dick couldn't bear to be touched. The pressure was insufferable. Poor Mr. Burns.

"We should go. I can't be late."

Jen grabbed her backpack and her car key. "I'll drive."

Letting Jen drive me to the office in her new Mini was my first mistake of the day. Conquest Broadcasting was a half-hour drive from my condo and could be more with the morning weekday traffic. It was getting worse by the day. Uncomfortable in the compact car, I squirmed, not used to sitting in a skirt, and I suddenly became aware of how itchy the wool fabric was, which made my dick feel worse than it already did. Needing as much legroom as I could get, I slid the passenger seat back as far as it would go.

"Buckle up, baby," ordered Jen as she started up the car.

"I can't," I groaned. "I don't think my dick can tolerate it."

Wordlessly, Jen glanced my way and buckled me in. At the click of the metal buckle, I yelped.

"Are you okay?" she asked.

"No!"

"You'll live, my poor baby," she said, driving out of the underground garage.

As we headed east on Wilshire, I had to keep adjusting my seat belt so it didn't hurt Mr. Burns. Every little jolt sent a cringe-worthy bolt of pain to my raging boner. How the hell was I going to make it through the board meeting? Let alone this drive?

I distracted myself with my iPhone, pretending to catch up on emails, but in truth, I was googling everything I could find on priapism. Today's second major mistake. Maybe the third, if you counted waking up. The more I read, the more I shuddered. Jen had not told me the worst-case scenario.

"Oh, my fucking God!" I cried out.

"Blake, what's the matter?" Her voice filled with alarm, my tiger took her eyes off the road and narrowly missed getting hit by a FedEx truck. Her tires screeched as she swerved into the left lane, and my fingertips dug into the leather seat, probably making dents.

Frankly, getting into an accident was nothing compared to the god-awful fate that awaited me. And I wasn't referring to the Board telling me to take a hike.

"You didn't tell me!"

"Tell you what?"

I read word for word from the WebMD article. *"Treatment of priapism may involve draining blood from the penis.* Jesus! They're going to have to put a needle into my cock!" Though I could slay a dragon for my wife, I was a chickenshit when it came to needles. It went back to my childhood and I could still remember bolting out of the doctor's office whenever I had to get a shot. Once I even tried to steal the needle and stick it in the doctor's eyes. That resulted in me having to see a child shrink until he offered money to my parents to send me to boarding school in Switzerland.

Jen was well aware of my morbid fear.

"Put your phone away! Reading about this condition isn't going to make things better."

She was right. It was making things worse. Way worse! Terror ripped through every fiber of my being, the phone shaking in my hand as I read more.

"And surgery may be necessary to prevent further damage! And I may have to have a shunt inserted! And did you read this? . . . *the longer you wait to see a*

doctor, the greater the chances of having irreversible damage! Permanent ED! Impotence! Holy Christ! What am I going to do?"

And if things couldn't get worse, I read this. *"In extreme cases, gonorrhea may set in and amputation may be necessary."* Oh my fucking God. The giant lump in my throat was like a wrecking ball. Kill me now.

Jen kept her eyes on the road, her fingers gripping the wheel. "Do you *really* have to go to the Board meeting?"

"YES! My father will blow a gasket if I don't show up."

"How long do they usually last?"

"They can go on for hours!" Panic filled every word. Every blood vessel. Every cell.

Jen blew out a shaky breath, and a tense silence saturated the air until we turned into the Conquest parking lot. Then, out of the blue, a wicked smile spread across my tiger's face as she pulled into her reserved parking spot. I'd seen that smile only once before—the time she'd come up with a plan to avenge Katrina after the psycho bitch had drugged and tried to rape me.

"Jen, what are you thinking?"

"I have an idea."

"What?"

She turned off the ignition. "You'll find out soon enough."

The twelve-member Board was already seated around my father's stately conference room table, bingeing on coffee and assorted pastries while looking over the agenda when I stepped into the room. Impeccably dressed in a silver gray power suit, he was at the head, the empty seat next to him waiting for me.

"Stay cool. Calm. And collected," I told myself as all eyes turned to me. My father's bushy brows shot up. He cleared his throat.

"Umm . . . Blake, did you by chance forget your bagpipes?"

The Board, which included three women, roared with laughter. "Nice legs," quipped one of them, which was followed by a pack of wolf whistles. So much for a bunch of so-called professionals. Scowling, my father did not look one iota pleased.

"Can you perhaps explain today's choice of outfit, son?"

Yeah, I've got a boner that could rival the Leaning Tower of Pisa and it's fucking killing me. And if I don't get the hell out of here soon, my dick may never be standing up straight again.

Not answering him, I took my designated seat and placed my laptop on the table in front of me, hooking it up to the slide projector while my father welcomed everyone and went over the agenda. The agenda was five pages long—running the gamut from our development slate to our bottom line. And first, we had to go over the minutes from the last forever-and-a-day meeting. Shitballs. We'd be here for hours. Maybe till after dinner. My heart sunk like the Titanic. I only wish my cock went down with it.

Yadda yadda yadda. Totally distracted by my throbbing dick, which barely made it under the table, I couldn't focus on a word my old man was saying. I had no clue how I was going to make it through my presentation, let alone this hellish day.

Suddenly, a quarter way through the agenda, a deafening alarm blasted through the room. Over the sound system came a commanding male voice: "Everyone please evacuate the building!"

The Board members leaped to their feet, scurrying to the door. My father and I did the same, following them out.

"What's going on?" I asked my dad, suppressing a groan. Jumping up like that was killer. I was in sheer agony.

"We must be having a fire drill," he replied, moving quickly down the hall with the Board members and hordes of other employees to our assigned emergency exit.

A few minutes later, we were all outside, gathered on the street. Another set of sirens blared in my ears and on the next blink of my eyes, dozens of blazing red fire engines were pulling up to the lot. Holy crap! Conquest Broadcasting might be on fire! Everything my father had worked for could go up in flames!

My eyes frantically searched the masses for Jennifer. My heart beating double time, I couldn't find her anywhere as the valiant firefighters, armed with axes and hoses, charged into the Conquest complex. The lot was vast . . . several acres that included office buildings, sound stages, postproduction studios, and trailers.

Though I didn't see any smoke or flames, panic surged inside me. My stomach knotted and my heart hammered. What if there *was* a real fire and Jen was trapped inside? Conquest Studios had once caught on fire before when I was thirteen, resulting in one unfortunate casualty. My tiger couldn't be the next!

Then, suddenly, a familiar slender hand gripped mine.

"Blake, let's go! We have a window of opportunity to get out of here."

A few short minutes later, we were back in her Mini, my tiger behind the wheel driving like a maniac. The speed limit was thirty-five, but she was driving twice over that. With every bump in the road, Mr. Burns silently cried out in agony.

"Jen! Slow down! We've got to go back! My father's company may be burning down!"

"It's not," she replied, her tone totally nonchalant.

"How do you know that?"

"Because I set the fire."

"What!?"

"It was just an itsy bitsy one in a wastebasket. I called it in anonymously . . . but put it out with some bottled water way before the fire department arrived." With a screech, she turned north onto busy Robertson Boulevard. "I told the 911 dispatcher that I saw someone set it. A guy in jeans and a hoodie. Arson!"

That description fit hundreds of Conquest employees. An investigation could take hours! Days! Weeks! A new frightening reality set in.

"Jen, if they investigate and discover you're behind this, you could go to jail!"

"They won't." The confidence in her voice assuaged my trepidation. "No one saw me."

"Are you sure?"

"Positive. A hundred percent positive."

I believed her . . . but still. "Tiger, wasn't there any alternative?"

"How else could we have broken up the Board meeting?"

I drew a blank. With my dick's existence at stake, my brain was in a thick fog. I glanced out the window, my surroundings a blur. "Where are we going?"

"To Cedars. You urgently need to be seen by a doctor."

"Why don't we just go to Dr. Klein's office? It's

right up the street and probably open now."

"I called his office, but he's out today. The nurse practitioner on duty said you need to go to the emergency room right away."

A shiver skittered down my spine. I hated hospitals. They were filled with sick people and my tiger had come close to dying in one once—Cedars, no less!

"We'll be there in no time," Jen beamed as the traffic suddenly came to a standstill. Up ahead of us, red lights were flashing. Police cars. It looked like three cars had rear-ended each other though I couldn't make out the extent of damage. The only damage I was focused on was the impending permanent damage to my cock. My heart raced as panic clawed at me. We had to get out of this clusterfuck before it was too late.

"Jen, what are we going to do? We're fucked!"

"Hold on!" Gripping the wheel, she cranked it to the right and with an ear-splitting screech, the car swerved onto a side street. Jesus. Was she also trying to give me whiplash?

A smug smile curled her lips. "Detour. We'll go up La Cienega instead and be there in no time."

Fingers crossed she was right.

For the first time in my life, I wanted my big fucking cock to be small.

Chapter 9

Blake

The emergency room was packed. Old and young alike hacking with coughs . . . moms holding wailing babies . . . kids howling with bloody knees . . . others sitting in wheelchairs looking like they were about to keel over . . . and more. How could so many people have life and death issues so early on a Tuesday morning in the middle of summer? None, however, could be as pressing (literally!) as mine. My throbbing cock was so heavy I thought it might snap off. I even glanced down at my feet, expecting to see a hard slab of flesh writhing on the floor until all life ebbed out of it.

"My husband has a medical emergency," Jen breathed out, her rapid-fire words coated with urgency.

Seated behind a Formica console in front of a large desktop computer, the frizzy-haired attendant on duty looked up at us, with a roll of her eyes. "So does everyone else here. What seems to be the problem?"

She eyed me up and down and dressed in my kilt, I felt myself cringe. Maybe she thought I was a cross-dresser who'd had some kind of psychotic break. Jen responded.

"His erection won't go down and he's in a lot of pain."

The woman, who had a nasal voice, flashed a snarky smile. "We haven't had one of those in a while. Sign in and take a seat. We'll call you when it's your turn to be seen."

"Do you know who I am?" I spat out, my clammy hands fisting by my sides.

"Yeah, a dude with a boner problem."

I clenched my jaw along with my hands so I wouldn't say or do something I'd regret. Like punching her in the face. Or squeezing her neck. Then, lucky for her, a distraction. Coming my way was a chubby little boy, about six or seven, with his mother. His wrist was encased in a lime green cast and he was sucking a matching color lollipop. He'd probably fallen off a jungle gym or something like that and fractured his arm. I'd done that once. My first of many visits to the emergency room. At the sight of me, the kid burst into hysterical laughter.

"Look, Mama!" he squealed, pointing a grubby little finger at me. "*That* man is wearing a skirt! That's so funny!"

It's not funny, you little brat. THAT MAN, for your information, is a gift to mankind. A superhero. I felt my blood simmering, my face reddening with rage. I was in grave pain; I didn't need more humiliation. For a brief moment, I thought about flashing my monstrous dick at him to give him something to cry about, but for obvious reasons I squashed that impulse. Instead, I stuck my tongue out at him and then smugly watched as his incensed mother dragged the shocked kid away by his good arm. *See ya, sucker. May you choke on your stupid lollipop and vomit up green shit.*

I celebrated my small victory with a mental air punch, but on my next breath, whatever red cape I was wearing in my head flew off into space. My attention returned to my dire situation and the hospital administrator.

"Do you need a wheelchair?" she asked, her beady eyes focused on my crotch.

A wheelbarrow was more like it. My throbbing cock felt like a block of concrete that some hardhat was drilling. "No," I grumbled as I scribbled my name on the sign-in sheet.

Frizzball gazed up at me. "Do you have insurance?"

"Yes, of course, I have insurance," I snipped.

"Can I please see your insurance card? And your I.D." Her tone was curt. "Well?"

Shit! In my haste to get out of the building when the fire alarm sounded, I'd left behind my computer bag, which contained my wallet with my insurance card, credit cards, driver's license, and a few hundred dollars.

"I'm with Aetna!" I gritted. "You can call them and

they'll verify it."

"I'm his wife and we both are," chimed in Jen. "Conquest Broadcasting, the company we both work for, insures us." Digging into her backpack, she produced her insurance card and flashed it.

The dubious administrator squinted at it. "Fine. Now, please take a seat. There are dozens of people ahead of you with their own emergencies. Some bigger than yours."

Was she kidding? There couldn't be an emergency bigger than mine, at least size-wise. I wanted to suffocate this bitch with my big dick. Shove it down her throat until she took her last breath.

"Next!" the woman bellowed, the line behind me having multiplied.

Jen hooked her arm in mine. "C'mon, Blake. Let's take a seat."

"No!" I refused to leave.

I hated to pull entitlement shit, but in my precarious situation, I had no choice. Fuck it! If Mr. Burns were to survive, I needed to be seen by a doctor immediately. Every second mattered. I looked at the pigheaded administrator straight in the eye, noting her nametag.

"Vilma, I happen to be Blake Burns . . . the son of Mr. and Mrs. Saul Bernstein . . . who happened to have donated the wing that is named after them. The Helen and Saul Bernstein Women's Pavilion. Does that ring a bell?"

Vilma looked at me blankly, then dismissively scrunched up her face. I don't think she believed a word I said, and it didn't help that I'd shortened my surname to Burns years ago. Rage was rising inside me like mercury; I was reaching my boiling point. As I was about to burst into a tirade, a familiar face joined us. Ughh! It was my sister's despicable ex, Matt, who like her was an OB-GYN. They'd once shared a thriving practice, but that had been dissolved, each now on their own. He raked his snakelike eyes over me.

"Isn't it a little early for Halloween?" he snickered.

God, I loathed him. And always had. I pressed my lips thin, wanting to rip his smarmy smile off his face.

"So, what brings you here, Blake?"

Something you should be suffering with, you two-timing prick. He had cheated on my sister with one of their blond bimbo patients, and their marriage had ended in a nasty divorce. It was actually a giant step forward for my sister and had brought us—and her twin boys—closer. Cemented us as family.

Narrowing my eyes, half in pain, half in contempt, I didn't answer him. Despising the piece of shit as much as I did, Jen jumped in.

"Matt, would you be kind enough to let the lovely Vilma here know that Blake is indeed the son of Helen and Saul Bernstein?"

"What's it worth to you?" What a fucking asshole! I had the burning urge to bash his balls in, and if I weren't in so much pain, I wouldn't have held back.

My brain wasn't functioning. Thank fuck, Jen's was.

"We'll take the boys over Christmas so you and Barbie can go away."

"Her name is Bambi," Matt sneered.

My brilliant Jen had remembered he had fought Marcy, wanting her to take care of the boys over the holidays so that he and his new bimbo whatever-the-fuck-her-name-was wife could go skiing in Aspen. His eyes lit up with score signs. Five minutes later, I was in a small, stark white examining room waiting to be seen. Jen hoisted herself up on the exam table and sat next to me, the sterile sheet of white paper rustling beneath us. She took my hand and entwined her lithe fingers with mine. Then, bowed her head, looking disheartened.

"Blake, I'm so sorry. This is all *my* fault. I should have never smeared that Dermadoo all over your penis." Her voice grew watery. "Can you ever forgive me?"

I squeezed her hand. "Look at me, baby." Her misty eyes met mine. "It's not your fault. You had no idea it would have this effect on me." I slid the leather pouch I was wearing to the side and noticed there was no sign of Mr. Burns deflating.

"But–"

I cut her off. "I let you. Besides, Ari Golden hinted at lunch that Dermadoo was some kind of sex enhancer, and Golden International was going to test-market it under another name. I was looking forward to using it." *Truth: I couldn't wait.*

"Really?"

"Really." I gave her a reassuring kiss on the top of her head.

My tiger quirked a faint, fleeting smile. Then her lush lips thinned and she again hung her head down. As if in shame. "I knew about its other 'benefits' too."

My eyebrows arched. "You did?"

She nodded, her expression forlorn. "Yes, from Chaz and Jeffrey. They couldn't stop raving about what it could do over lunch." She paused. "I'm sorry, my love. So, so sorry."

I gently tipped up her chin with my thumb and turned her head to face me. I looked her straight in the eye. "Stop it, Jen. There's no need to apologize. It's a weird, freak thing. Let it go."

Her expression lightened a bit, but she still wore a look of regret. "You must have had some kind of extreme allergic reaction to it."

"Yeah."

"Does it still hurt, baby?"

"Yeah, a lot." *A whole fucking lot.*

"Can I take a peek at it?"

"Okay." My voice was hesitant. I wasn't sure. Make that, I was afraid. Fear trickled right down to my balls, but just in time, there was a knock at the door. My eyes flitted to the handle as it turned. The door swung open, and a stout older man in a white lab coat moseyed in. He was carrying a clipboard and wearing a stethoscope around his neck. With his wiry white hair that stuck out from his temples and bulging electron green eyes, he reminded me a lot of the Christopher Lloyd character in those *Back to the Future* movies.

"Hello! I'm Dr. Boris Cocker."

Dr. Cocker? Seriously?

Behind him trailed a buxom nurse with a beehive blond hairdo and blood red lips, wheeling a cart full of gizmos.

"And this is Nurse Needles."

Jesus! Nurse Needles? Were they putting me on?

The scary-looking woman shot me a wicked smile, exposing her razor-sharp incisors as she lifted a syringe to her eyes and examined it. "We're all set, doctor," she cackled, her gaze as pointed as the sharp, jutting six-inch needle. *I'll get you and your big dick too!* Holy shit! At the sight of it, cold fear washed over me. I gulped and my heart almost stopped. If only this was a bad dream, but it wasn't.

My terrified gaze moved back to the doctor as he read over his notes. "So I understand we have a little bit of a problem here." The corners of his thin lips curled up into a sadistic grin.

"I would call it more of a big problem." I quivered as Jen slid off the exam table and took a seat on the chair in the corner.

"Can I stay, doctor? I'm his wife."

"Don't leave me, tiger," I mentally cried out as the words of the WebMD article collided in my brain. My fear morphed into into panic. The big needle is coming! Then the knife!

"Of course, Mrs. Burns."

Goodbye forever, Mr. Burns. My pending, unthinkable loss filled my every thought as the doctor and nurse took my vitals. A shiver skated down my spine and my heart thudded as the doctor relayed the results.

"Your blood pressure is slightly elevated . . ."

Slightly?

"But that's to be expected. Everything else seems normal."

Another insidious smile. I swear that the art of the reassuring smile was a part of every doctor's med school curriculum. A requirement. Cocker had for sure taken the advanced course: *Smiling 501: Dude, Your Life is Over.*

"So let's take a look-see, shall we?"

My seven-year-old voice screamed in my head. *Run, Blake, run! Get the crap out of here!* Except, shaking from head to toe, I was too paralyzed with fear to jump off the table and sprint out of the room as the mad doctor expertly undid the three-inch safety pin fastening my kilt.

"Nice plaid," he commented. "A Buchanan." *Jen's*

mother's maiden name. "Our side of the Cocker clan can be traced back to eleventh century Scotland. Our family plaid is a Black Watch. I wear my kilt to every family gathering. It drives my wife crazy . . . I mean in a good way. Say, have you ever been to Scotland?"

In freak-out mode, I was in no mood for small talk. Jen answered. "We haven't, but my parents went earlier this year and loved it. They brought Blake back this kilt."

"Good for them!" the doctor beamed as he removed the gold pin. Setting it on the table, he slowly opened the flap of the skirt and blew out a breath as his eyes landed on my exposed organ and widened.

"Whoa!"

My heart beat like a jackhammer. "Is that a good 'whoa' or a bad one?"

"Just a big one." His eyes narrowing, he studied my cock. "Do you mind if I touch it a bit?"

"Do you seriously have to?" I sure as hell didn't want some crazy ass doctor poking around my dick.

"Yes, it's an important part of the examination." My eyes stayed trained on his hands as they performed a pat down on my rigid shaft, as if Mr. Burns was a criminal and concealing some kind of weapon.

"Ow!" I yelped as he ran his fingers over a particularly sensitive spot.

My empathetic tiger scrunched her face. Angst etched all over it. "Doctor, please be gentle. My husband is in a lot of pain."

That was an understatement. My cock was raging! Bursting at the seams! It was going to implode!

"I can see that," said the doctor as his dexterous hands moved toward the crown. He squeezed the tip, causing me to wince yet again. Fucking sadist!

"Well, I know now which type of priapism you have," he stated, taking his hands off my cock.

My brows shot up. "There are different kinds?" In my mind, I already knew the answer: the kind that can kill you and the kind that can't. I was positive I had the former. Before long, both my cock and I would be ancient history. A feeling of impending doom pulsed through me. I felt lightheaded, sick to my stomach, as the doctor continued.

"Your penile shaft is rigid, but the tip is soft, leading me to believe you have the most common kind. Ischemic."

"Ischemic?"

"Yes. Low flow priapism . . . the result of blood being trapped and unable to leave the penis."

Trapped? While every nerve in my body crackled with fear, the scary man in the white coat began to ask me a series of questions, writing down my responses on his clipboard. Was I on meds for any condition? Had my penis sustained any recent trauma? Had I ever been diagnosed with sickle cell anemia, leukemia, or diabetes? Was I on any kind of antidepressant, blood thinner, or hormone? Had I recently been bit by a spider? Did I ever experience erectile dysfunction?

The answer to every question was a terse no . . . the decibel of my voice rising until I was shouting out the answer to the final question so loudly the walls shook. I wasn't going to tell him about the Katrina drug-induced impotence incident. It didn't count!

"Doc, I'm dying here. Can't you just unbig me?"

"Just one more question . . . did you and your wife engage in sexual intercourse last night?"

"YES! We fucked like bunnies, if you honestly need to know."

Jen's face turned a deep shade of crimson. "Dr. Cocker, we made love for hours and used a lubricant. A new-to-us moisturizer."

Cocker cocked a brow. "Can you tell me the name of the product?"

"Dermadoo."

Evil Nurse Needles, who had been a quiet observer all this time, suddenly lit up. "Dermadoo!! My husband and I use it all the time! The best sex ever!"

The doctor pivoted to face her. "Did he ever have this reaction?"

"Actually, once. And it came along with an asthma attack. With a half hour of icing and a few whoofs of his inhaler—badda bing!—his erection went down and he was back to being his normal, horny self." Flashing that frightening overbite smile, she made a circle with her left thumb and index finger and inserted the needle held in her right hand in and out of it. Pumping it faster and faster. Getting off on it. Me, wishing she would stop. The vision of her poking the needle into my cock was vivid in my mind. I silently screamed. *Please, stop!*

"Interesting." The doctor turned back to face me as Nurse Needles finally ceased her needle-fest. "Excuse me, Blake. Sit tight while I text my brother, Morris. He's a proctologist."

Seriously? There were two *alta cocker* Cocker doctors—Boris and Morris—and one actually specialized in cocks and balls? Anxiety crawled back inside me like an army of ants as I watched the doctor pull out his phone from one of his lab coat pockets. His nimble thumbs texted deftly. I wondered what he was typing. He hit send and a ping sounded shortly. His brother had responded. And then one more round of back and forth texts.

Mad Nurse Needles held up the monstrous needle again, her venomous eyes aglow. "Doctor, should I prepare to aspirate?"

Over my dead body! Visions of last night's nightmare flashed in my head. I was going to lose Mr. Burns for good! My cock was a goner! A nauseating mixture of adrenaline and apprehension zipped through my bloodstream. I was ready to leap off the exam table and make a mad dash out of the room when the doctor responded.

"Nurse, no need to numb and aspirate. Let's try

icing and a dose of terbutaline."

"Injectable?"

Gah! Another needle!

"No, let's do oral. My brother thinks it could work."

One hour later, I was hugging Dr. Cocker and Nurse Needles. My former nemeses were now my new best friends! Thanks to a half hour of icing and a dose of terbutaline, my dick, though a little sore, had returned to normal. It had unbigged! I wanted to mentally high-five it but didn't dare, thinking it might rise to attention again.

Ready to check out of the ER, I had my marching orders. I had to take warm baths nightly, be on ter-bulatine for five days, and refrain from sexual intercourse for a week. Under any other circumstances, I would have protested the no-sex edict, but I was thankful to have my dick back to normal at any cost. Oh yeah, I also had to wear an elastic constrictor around Mr. Burns—kind of like a brace to keep him in place. It was terribly uncomfortable, but hell, if it was going to help regulate my cock I was game.

"Doc, what's the long-term prognosis?" I asked before leaving the hospital.

"I'd say it's looking good."

Thank fuck, the irony of the two words I said to myself not lost on me.

"Say hello to your parents for me, Blake." Then, a wink. "Oh, and be sure to wear your kilt more often."

Chapter 10

Blake

Conquest Broadcasting was closed for the rest of the day. With a possible arsonist still on the loose, the LAFD had told my father it was too risky to keep employees on the lot. The search would last through the night. Hence, everyone was given the day off and high-level executives were urged to take all important meetings off-site. Instead of reconvening the Board meeting at a different location, my father invited all the members to his palatial Beverly Hills house to play golf. With no reason to head back to the office, Jen and I drove home to our condo. After my ordeal, I was glad to be home. And stay home. Worn-out Mr. Burns needed bed rest. But I needed something more.

"Thanks for being there for me, tiger," I said for the umpteenth time as she heated up the matzo ball soup we'd picked up at Nate 'n Als on the way home. "That was scary. I don't know how I would have made it without you."

I was now casually dressed in loose-fitting sweats

and a UCLA Bruins T-shirt and barefoot. Her hair gathered in a high ponytail, Jen was wearing a pair of my cotton boxer shorts and a cropped top that exposed her long, toned legs and taut abs. On her feet were her favorite Ugg slippers. Pink and furry. Damn, she looked cute! So fuckable. Mr. Burns thought so too. I fought my erection. Yeah, Mr. Burns and I were in a wrestling match and I had to hold him down. The stupid brace wasn't helping much.

As the battle between my legs raged, Jen spun around and met my gaze. Holding a big wooden spoon in her hand, which I found crazily erotic, she said, "My love, I'll always be there for you."

I drew her closer to me, wrapping my arms around her tiny waist. "Tiger, I have to ask you a question." Her eyes melted into mine and I paused. "If I lost my manhood . . ."

"What do you mean?"

"I mean if I got permanent ED and I could never have an erection again and fuck you properly—and give you multiple orgasms—would you still love me?"

She furrowed her brows, looking taken aback. "Blake, what kind of question is that?"

"A long, hard one."

"Well, the answer, not at all like your cock, is short and sweet: Of course!"

I was stunned into silence as she continued.

"Blake, we took a vow. To love each other in sickness and health. You've loved me every way possible, even knowing I might have life-threatening cancer and not be capable of giving you a child, and I'm committed to doing the same."

"But that's different."

"How is it different?" she challenged.

"Because I couldn't live without you no matter what the circumstances."

Setting the spoon on the kitchen counter, her arms flew around my neck.

"Blake, in case you don't remember, I didn't marry you for your cock though I must say it's pretty spectacular."

"Just *pretty* spectacular?" I asked, feigning hurt.

"No. Amazingly . . . incredibly . . . unbelievably . . . mind-blowingly. But you're missing the point."

"The point being . . ."

Her hands moved to my face, cupping my cheeks, and with a tilt of her head, she looked deep into my eyes. "Blake, I married you for you. For *all* of you. Most of all for your big, beautiful heart, which fills every fiber of my being every second of the day. Because I love *you* so, so much."

My heart was melting. Turning into goo. Ready to pour into the empty sixteen-ounce soup container on the counter.

Her hands still cradling my face, I leaned in to give her a hot, passionate kiss, and as our mouths and tongues connected, an unsavory smell wafted up my nose. Jen smelled it too and broke away. Holy shit! The matzo ball soup was burning! The chicken broth had totally evaporated and the two big doughy balls were sizzling. Just like mine.

"Oh my God," we screamed in unison. Acting fast, Jen beat me to turning off the flame of the gas stove.

"Phew!" she exhaled.

I drew her into me again. "You *are* an arsonist!"

She laughed, holding me tight. "And *you're* on fire."

She was right! I was on major fire. I was so hot, so hungry for her I thought I would combust.

With the possibility of burning down the building over, I lifted Jen onto the kitchen counter. I nuzzled her neck, tasting her sweetness, and inhaled the intoxicating cherry-vanilla scent of her hair, which increased both my appetite and libido. Which could be one and the same.

"Jen, baby, I'm starving for you."

"But, Blake," she moaned, "Dr. Cocker said you can't have sex until next week."

I rolled my tongue down the slender column of her neck, arousing her further, while a hand moved beneath the waistband of the boxers. My fingers crept down to her caressable triangle. God, she was so hot and wet for me.

"Tiger, maybe we can't fuck, but I still can do a lot

to you. I haven't eaten all day and I'm ravenous."

Still flicking her neck with my tongue, I slid down the boxers until they fell to the floor and then went down on her, burying my head between her thighs. I kissed. I licked. I sucked. I tongue fucked.

"Do you like Mr. T?" The words barely left my mouth. God, she tasted so good! To me, like honey.

"You mean that gold-chained action hero from *The A-Team*?" Her voice was breathless and enraptured. "That show was dumb." Jen had a Master's Degree in media studies from USC's prestigious film school and knew every TV series there was from television's beginning.

I flicked her clit with the tip. "No, I mean this Mr. T . . . my tongue. He's substituting for my cock while he's on hiatus." Then I sucked her clit hard, eliciting a loud moan.

"Oh, yes! He's doing a fine job!"

I spread her legs wider, putting her Ugg-covered feet on my broad shoulders. Not losing oral contact with her swollen, pulsing clit, I plunged my middle finger into her pussy and began to pump her. Faster and harder. Gripping the edge of the granite counter, my tiger flung her head back. Her breaths were coming out in gasps and soon she was whimpering.

"Oh my God, Blake! This is too much for me! I need to come!"

She began to buck against both my tongue and digit,

and I wish I had an extra set of hands to keep her from falling off the counter. She was falling apart.

Beneath my sweats, I could feel Mr. Burns trying to burst out of my stupid cock brace. Fuck me. How was I going to make it through the week without being able to penetrate her? Come inside her? Come in her mouth? Come in her ass? Come in her hands? Hell, I wasn't even allowed to masturbate and come in my own hands.

And then, my tiger roared.

And every selfish thought evaporated.

She was all I needed. All I wanted.

"I love you so much, baby!"

"The same."

With the sweet taste of her still on my tongue, I held her impassioned face between my hands and kissed her madly.

Chapter 11

Jennifer

Almost One Week Later

I must have been dreaming of visiting Scotland with Blake. Bagpipes droned in my ears, their soulful melody rousing me. I forced my eyes halfway open. No, I wasn't dreaming. I could still hear them.

"Blake, do you hear that?" I murmured, my voice groggy. We'd been out late last night with our friends Gloria and Jaime Zander to celebrate the signed Dermadoo deal. Neither of us mentioned our nightmarish experience with the moisturizer, and whether Gloria and Jaime had had better luck with the product than we did was never discussed. We all got a little smashed and when we got home, my husband had the munchies and ravenously ate me out. Since our terrifying ordeal, we still hadn't fucked, but I couldn't complain about the attention Blake was lavishing on me. I honestly didn't know how he kept his dick intact. Pure willpower or maybe that ridiculous cock brace helped.

No response from Blake. I rolled over onto my side, thinking he must be fast asleep. To my surprise, he wasn't there. Though it was Sunday, the one day we usually slept in, maybe he'd gotten up early and gone for a jog or to Starbucks. The bagpipes continued to chime in my ears. Sitting up, I was about to amble over to our bedroom window to see what was happening on the street below when a chipper voice that sounded much like Blake's caught me by surprise.

"Good mornin', m'lady! I have brought *ye* breakfast in bed."

My eyes shot to our bedroom door where Blake, wearing his kilt, a T-shirt, and a megawatt smile, stood barefoot. Between his hands was a silver tray with a full tea service and a plate full of delectable pastries. There was also a greeting card standing smack in the middle.

As I lowered the fluffy duvet and got into a cross-legged position, Blake swaggered my way. "So, m' lady, I want to know . . . do *ye* still think I look like a sexy warrior in a kilt?"

"Is that a trick question?" I replied, my lips curling into a seductive smile.

"No, it's a straightforward one. *Aye?*"

I didn't respond, noticing he wasn't wearing the traditional leather pouch that accompanied the kilt. Not wearing my glasses, my morning vision was blurry, but I was almost positive—though not a 100% sure—there was a substantial bulge beneath the pleated plaid fabric.

Setting the tray down on my night table, he plucked the card and crawled onto the bed, sitting cross-legged in front of me. The front of the card featured an adorable Scottish terrier with a red tartan collar and the word "Woof!" Opening it, my husband began to read aloud in his perfect Scottish accent. I often forgot that Blake could have been a great actor, but this reminded me.

"Oh Jenny's wet, poor body,

Jenny's seldom dry:

She dragged all her petticoat

Coming through the rye!

If a body met a body

Coming through the rye,

If a body kissed a body,

Need a body cry?

If a body met a body

Coming through the glen,

If a body kissed a body

Need the world know?"

"You wrote this, baby?" I asked, somewhat incredu-lously. My husband, who'd once wrote silly limericks, now wrote beautiful poetry, his first unforgettable poem being the one he recited the third and final time we exchanged wedding vows at my parents' house in July. My surprise Christmas in July wedding.

"Wishful thinking, m'love," he replied with an eye roll, his voice still accented. "I borrowed and adapted it from a book *yur* father bought me in Scotland. The greatest poems of another gifted Burns . . . *Robert.*"

Robert Burns, best known for "Auld Lang Syne," was one of my father's favorite poets, and he'd once taught a course on him when he was an English professor at Des Moines University. It moved me that my dad had instilled Blake with a love for poetry and that they often spent time together analyzing certain verses.

Blake set the card down on the bed, and a devilish smile crossed his lips.

"So, m'lady, shall we enjoy breakfast in bed?"

My eyes darted to the tray of tea and pastries. "What are those?"

"Scones. I had them flown here from Scotland."

"Wow! They look delicious. Do you want to share one?"

Blake glanced at the tray and then met my gaze. "Maybe later, but right now I want *ye* to devour the very special one I've brought *ye*."

"What do you mean?"

Before I could blink an eye, he flashed his kilt. Beneath it stood his cock. Commando. And for the first time in almost a week, unsheathed by the protective brace. And fully erect! It was very big. Let me rephrase. Very, very big! So thick and rigid! And along it was a thin layer of white frosting and on the crown, a creamy bead of pre-cum.

"Breakfast in bed, m'love."

I was so turned on. So hungry for him! My watering mouth hadn't been near his beautiful cock for almost seven long days. I was going to make this a breakfast neither of us would forget.

"Oh, Blake, it looks so yum!" I was going to start with the cum and work my tongue up and down his length. Then, I was going to take him in my mouth and suck him dry.

Getting onto my knees, I planted my hands on his muscular thighs for support and, lowering my head, flicked my tongue on the beaded tip.

"Oh yeah," I heard my warrior murmur as my vessel proceeded to trail along his iced shaft, licking off every bit of the vanilla-flavored frosting.

"Mmm," I moaned, the salty-sweet flavor filling my mouth. "So yum."

"*Yer* so yum," Blake moaned back. "I'm going to watch *ye* devour my special scone."

On my trip back up, I rolled my tongue around the tip, then licked my lips before clamping my wet, hungry mouth around the wide crown. Blake groaned with pleasure.

"Oh, m'tiger, the things that sweet, pretty mouth of

yers can do!"

I'd only just begun to show him. On my next hot breath, I went down on him, taking his cock in my mouth all the way. Blake hissed and I could feel the rippled muscles of his thighs tense.

"Fuck, baby!"

On cue, I began to devour his cock with my mouth. Moving one hand to the base, my mouth bobbed up and down his hard, thick, delicious length, picking up speed and adding pressure—and pleasure—with each determined pilgrimage. In tandem, my hand pumped the base, squeezing hard. I began to hum something that sounded like "Auld Lang Syne" as Blake's shallow breaths joined the sensuous bagpipes, which were still playing outside. I glanced up once at Blake—his head was tilted back and an expression of tortured ecstasy was etched on his face. It was all so unbelievably erotic. I was so turned on, wetness pooling between my thighs and tingles dancing in my belly. Blake's cock filled the hollows of my cheeks and I thought any second he would blow. Then, as I felt the telltale vibrations, he pulled out of me and on my next heartbeat, I was flat on my back. In one swift move, he yanked off my boy shorts and then undid his kilt, tossing them both to the floor. With a powerful thrust of one knee, he spread my legs and ordered me to wrap them around him as he anchored himself above me. His magnificent sculpted body grazed mine, his breath blowing in my face like a warm highland breeze.

"Tiger, if *ye* thought I was going to come in *yer* mouth, *ye* were wrong. I've waited all week to come inside *ye*." My pulse sped up as he caressed me. "M'love, repeat after me . . . Oh, Jenny's so wet."

Breathily, I did as he asked—oh God, was I!—my wet arousal, my need for him so intense. "So wet," I repeated deliriously as he sunk his colossal cock inside me with ease because, in all honesty, I was drenched to the core.

"*Aye*, so wet and ready for me," he murmured, taking me to the hilt. "Aah, m'tiger! *Ye* feel so fuckin' good. I've missed *ye* so much."

"The same," I moaned, my ache for him so great. "The same."

And then he began to pummel me. In and out. Harder and faster. The strokes long and determined, like he was sprinting to win a marathon. And couldn't wait to get to the finish line.

"Baby, I'm not going to last long," he managed between thrusts and grunts.

"Me either."

A few moments later, we were both coming through the rye.

After our breathing returned to normal, we were lying on our backs, Blake's arm draped around me, my head on his chest, our eyes shut, our hearts beating as one in amorous bliss. Oh, how I loved my warrior! My lover! My protector! *That* man!

From this day onward, kinky kilt sex became part of our weekly rituals. And at the end of the month, he surprised me with a ticket to Scotland and a promise to fuck me until all my ancestors awoke and heard me roar his name.

A NOTE FROM BLAKE

Hey there, all you beautiful readers~

Man, that was fucking scary. I was scared shitless. Or should I say dickless. You may be laughing now, but it wasn't funny then.

Can you imagine how different my life with Jen would have been if I'd gotten permanent ED? I would have let her down forever, no pun intended.

Thank fuck, all is well now. Dr. Cocker (Morris, not Boris) is my new proctologist. I've gone to see him a few times since the crisis and he's assured me Mr. Burns is in tiptop shape. He's still uncertain what caused the bout of priapism. It could have been the Dermadoo or maybe it was just a freak random thing. One thing for sure is neither Jen nor I are going near that stuff for as long as we live. I don't even want it on my fingertips. I'll sacrifice fine lines around my eyes for worry-free procreation. We gave the rest of the case Ari Golden had given us to Chaz and Jeffrey with no explanation except that we didn't need it. Sex with my tiger—without it—couldn't be better.

As always, some good came out of the bad. The

best being that my potential ED proved to me yet again how much my tiger loves me. Unconditionally, with her body, heart, and soul. Even if I could never get it up again, she'd stay by my side. And love me for who I am. Forever and an eternity.

I promised her a trip to Scotland, and we went at the end of September. I wanted to stay in a famous castle; she wanted to stay in a cozy village inn. We ended up doing both, the first just outside Edinburgh, the latter in the heart of the Scottish Highlands.

I wore my kilt the entire time commando and bought Jen a mini-skirted version of mine. She looked so damn cute in it and I wanted to fuck her everywhere we went. Bend her over and lift up that little skirt and fuck her hard from behind. Or slip my hand under the front panel and finger her while we were driving around the countryside or listening to some tour guide lecture about the sights. One night, after fucking her senseless, I got inspired and pulled out my pen. And found a sheet of paper.

There once was a lad in a kilt
Who took his lass to the hilt.
She roared his name when she came
Till it was heard in Spain
And that's how the legend of *That Man* was built.

Okay, so not every poem can be a masterpiece. I admit it needs work and is not going to win the Robert Burns prize for best romantic poem. But I'm working on it.

Until next time . . .
I.T.A.L.Y.~ Blake

PS. In case you don't remember, I.T.A.LY. stands for *I Totally Always Love You*. And yeah, I do.

A NOTE FROM NELLE

Dearest Reader~

I so hope you loved reading this novella as much as I loved writing it. And I hope it put a big smile on your face and made you laugh aloud in these challenging times. It would mean the world to me if you wrote a review on Amazon or wherever you purchased or downloaded it. It can be as long or as short as you wish. Regardless of length, your reviews help others discover my books.

This is the first in a series of books I plan to write, which revolve around the first years of Blake and his tiger's marriage as well as their friends and family members. It's so much fun writing about them as a married couple!

Coming up next and very soon . . . *THAT MAN 8*. This is a full-length standalone novel and I'm totally in love with it! It has lots of steamy sex, laugh out loud moments, some nail-biting suspense plus a touch of tenderness that brought tears to my eyes! Grandma's in it too! And wait till you meet the latest—and cutest— addition to Blake and Jen's family. To get you excited, I'm including the first two chapters and a Pre-Order link.

As always, my Belles, thank you from the bottom of my heart for your love and support! Please stay safe and healthy! Don't hesitate to drop me an email to say hello. I'd love to hear from you and will personally respond. You are the reason I write!

With all my love and appreciation . . .
MWAH! ~ Nelle ♥

THAT MAN 8
Nelle L'Amour

Chapter 1

Jennifer

Click.

"Blake, do you hear that?" I whispered, fear creeping into my bones. My heart pounded against my ribs. And my chest constricted.

Just home from our amazing trip to Scotland, in time for my twenty-sixth birthday, I'd tossed and turned for hours, unable to fall asleep. I was suffering from jet lag. I anxiously glanced at the clock on my nightstand—it was only ten p.m., but in Scotland, it was six o'clock in the morning. Almost time to wake up.

I heard another barely audible click. It sounded like it was coming from the door to our condo—like the deadbolt was unlocking. Someone was trying to break in! I was positive!

"Blake!" I repeated, my voice rising over his light snoring. He was sound asleep, his chest gently rising and falling. I swear my husband could sleep through a 9.0 earthquake unlike me who was a light sleeper because of the deep-seated anxiety I still harbored. Someone had tried to rape me when I was in college . . . and that someone—a deranged game show producer— had tried to kill me shortly after I joined Conquest Broadcasting and would have had not Blake showed up—just in the nick of time—and stopped him. Don Springer was out of my life for good, and while I'd gone into therapy after the harrowing life and death experience and taken a course in self-defense, I was still traumatized by the slightest disturbance.

"Blake, wake up!!" I said in my loudest hushed voice, nudging his shoulder.

He shifted in the bed, pulling the duvet up to his chin. "What's going on?" he murmured, his voice groggy and his eyes still glued shut.

"Listen! Do you hear that?" The rattling sound was unmistakable. The front door had been opened. We were being robbed! I bolted upright, a cold shudder running down my spine.

Consciousness slowly filled Blake. His long-lashed eyelids fluttered, then blinked open. His irises glowed midnight blue in the darkness. Pulling down the covers, he pushed himself up to a sitting position.

"Blake, someone's in the house!"

"Shh!" Light footsteps thudded in our ears, fol- lowed by the clatter of drawers and cabinets slamming open and shut. The frightening reality finally sank into my husband. "Shit!" Wearing not a stitch of clothing, he jumped out of bed. My eyes trained on his beautiful sculpted body—that gorgeous hard as rock ass and long muscular legs—as he hurried to his walk-in closet.

"Blake, what are you doing?"

"Shh! Be quiet and stay still! I'm getting a weapon!"

A weapon? Given that we lived in a luxury, high-security doorman building, we didn't keep a gun in the apartment. Even after the incident at my former duplex. The closest thing we had was a set of butcher knives in the kitchen. And my pepper spray, which was likewise in the kitchen in my backpack. But those weren't going to help.

My heart beating double time, I watched as Blake opened the closet door and re-emerged with a long stick in one hand and the other gripped around a small object I couldn't discern.

"What are you holding?"

"My little league baseball bat!" He held it up, flexing his pronounced bicep as he brandished it and then tossed me the small object. With a thump, it landed on the bed close to me.

"What's this?" I whispered, reaching for the small shiny object.

"My Swiss Army Boy Scout knife."

Under normal circumstances, I would have playfully challenged my husband's claim to being a Boy Scout—*Boy Scout's honor*—but this was hardly the time. Our lives were in danger.

"Hold on to it and call 911!" Gripping the bat, he tiptoed toward our bedroom door.

"Blake, I'm scared! Be careful!"

Without wasting a second, I grabbed my phone and called 911.

Chapter 2

Blake

My heart beat like a jackrabbit's as I stealthily crept down the dark hallway that led to the living room. Every nerve was on edge, every sense on high alert. There were more footsteps in the near distance, and then what sounded like dishes and silverware clambering. We were definitely being robbed!

Breathing in and out of my nose, I gripped my bat tighter, willing myself to stay rational and in the moment. My mind swam with questions and worst-case scenarios. What if the burglar had a knife or a gun? What if he attacked me? Took me by surprise? And maybe there were two of them! More than anything, I hoped my tiger, whom I loved more than life itself—the woman I would slay dragons for—would be safe. Shit! I forgot to tell her to lock the bedroom door, but now it was too late. Naked as I was, I mentally donned my red cape. I was *That Man*, her superhero and protector.

In my head, I formed a plan of attack. The room

pitch black, I would sneak up on the perpetrator and before he had a chance to hear or see me, I'd bash him over the head with the bat or take a swing at him if he dared to make a move on me. Either way, knock him out, kick in his balls for good measure, and then tie him up while waiting for the police to arrive. Fingers crossed they were already on the way and soon sirens would be wailing in my ears.

Armed with my bat and my plan, I tried to steady my shaky breaths as I stepped foot into the living room. Suddenly, the overhead lights flashed on. I blinked once and let out a startled scream.

And so did *she!*

WANT TO FIND OUT WHO'S BROKEN INTO BLAKE AND JEN'S CONDO? Pre-Order *THAT MAN 8!* The steamiest, funniest, and most heartwarming installment of the *THAT MAN* series! A full-length novel that'll make you laugh, cry and swoon!

THAT MAN 8

**COMING ON
OCTOBER 15, 2020
PREORDER NOW**

ACKNOWLEDGMENTS

First and foremost, I'd like to thank my dear writer friend, Adriane Leigh, for giving me the brilliant idea to continue Blake and his tiger's story. I'll never forget that morning over our churro breakfast in Mexico City, following a writer's conference, where we were brainstorming and she came up with it. I am totally beholden and please do check out her books. They're amazing! She also writes short steamy novellas under the pen name Aria Cole.

Next let me thank my fabulous group of betas, whom I also love as friends. They include: Kelly Green, Marti Jentis, Jill Johnson, Kristen Myers, Ilene Rosen, Lisa Sanders, Mary Jo Toth, and Joanna Halliday-Warren. I am so thrilled you loved *THAT MAN 7* and fell in love all over again with scorchin' hot Blake Burns. And found my deliciously flawed alpha hero as hilarious as ever.

Another big shout-out goes to my crew . . .

Arijani Karčić, my fabulous cover designer who created what would become an iconic cover. LOL! I hope we don't run out of colors as there will be plenty more *THAT MAN* books. You are the best!

Hayfaah S., my extremely talented teaser and graphics designer. Love you!

Virginia Tesi Carey, my eagle-eye proofreader, who catches my typos and also helps me figure out prepositions I never get right.

Paul Salvette/BBebooks, my always patient and there-for-me formatter.

Candi Kane, for organizing my Release Blitz and for being so patient with me.

Kelly Green, my invaluable PA who keeps my head on straight.

My A-Team, my dear group of supportive writer friends whose names all begin with the letter "A" . . . Auden Dar, A.M Hargrove, Adriane Leigh, Angel Payne, Arianne Richmonde, and Aleatha Romig. I love you all! And do check out their books! You'll be thanking me!

Finally, a big thank you to my family for putting up with me and affording me the opportunity to write. I love you guys and owe you lots of dinners!

Stay well all!!

MWAH! ~ Nelle ♥

BOOKS BY NELLE L'AMOUR

Secrets and Lies

Sex, Lies & Lingerie

Sex, Lust & Lingerie

Sex, Love & Lingerie

Unforgettable

Unforgettable Book 1

Unforgettable Book 2

Unforgettable Book 3

THAT MAN Series

THAT MAN 1

THAT MAN 2

THAT MAN 3

THAT MAN 4

THAT MAN 5

THAT MAN 6

THAT MAN 7

THAT MAN 8

Alpha Billionaire Duet
TRAINWRECK 1
TRAINWRECK 2

Love Duet
Undying Love
Endless Love

A Standalone Romantic Comedy
Baby Daddy

A Second Chance Romantic Suspense Standalone
Remember Me

An OTT Insta-love Standalone
The Big O

A Romance Compilation
Naughty Nelle

ABOUT THE AUTHOR

I am a *New York Times* and *USA Today* bestselling author who lives in Los Angeles with her Prince Charming-ish husband, twin college-age princesses, and a bevy of royal pain-in-the-butt pets. A former executive in the entertainment industry with a prestigious Humanitas Prize for promoting human dignity and freedom to my credit, I gave up playing with Barbies a long time ago, but I still enjoy playing with toys with my hubby. While I write in my PJs, I love to get dressed up and pretend I'm Hollywood royalty. My steamy stories feature characters that will make you laugh, cry, and swoon and stay in your heart forever. They're often inspired by my past life.

To learn about my new releases, sales, and giveaways, please sign up for my newsletter and follow me on social media. I love to hear from my readers.

Website:
www.nellelamour.com

Newsletter:
nellelamour.com/newsletter

Nelle's Belles:
facebook.com/groups/1943750875863015

Facebook:
facebook.com/NelleLamourAuthor

Instagram:
instagram.com/nellelamourauthor

Twitter:
twitter.com/nellelamour

Amazon:
amazon.com/Nelle-LAmour/e/B00ATHR0LQ

BookBub:
bookbub.com/authors/nelle-l-amour

Email:
nellelamour@gmail.com

Printed in Great Britain
by Amazon